Praise for Charlie Cochrane's
Lessons in Desire

"...a highly entertaining reading experience. I think I'm hooked on these books now. If book three in this series maintains the high standard that Ms. Cochrane has set so far with her Cambridge Fellows Mysteries series, then it promises to be a winner as well. I look forward to my next visit with Stewart and Coppersmith and wonder what situation they could possibly get into next."

~ *Fallen Angel Reviews*

"The second book in the Cambridge Fellows series is another wonderfully lyrical story that engages the reader with the slow pace of life in the early 1900s. This beautiful writing, clever mystery, touches of humor, and engaging characters create an interesting story that never sacrifices the pace and time for quick action or sex scenes. ...Be sure to pick up this story when you want an easy, languid journey filled with gentle laughter, love, and a touch of very English mystery. The lovely prose and delightful characters carry the book when the action is light."

~ *Whipped Cream Reviews*

Look for these titles by *Charlie Cochrane*

Now Available:

Lessons in Desire

A Cambridge Fellows Mystery

Charlie Cochrane

A Samhain Publishing, Ltd. publication.

Samhain Publishing, Ltd.
577 Mulberry Street, Suite 1520
Macon, GA 31201
www.samhainpublishing.com

Cover by Scott Carpenter

First Samhain Publishing, Ltd. electronic publication: August 2009
First Samhain Publishing, Ltd. print publication: July 2010

Dedication

This book is inspired by all the holidays I've spent on my favorite island. Jersey is unique, a very special place, although I've taken liberties with some of its geography.

I dedicate this to all the girls on the good ship Naughty who've proved such great friends.

Chapter One

St. Bride's College, Cambridge, June 1906

"A holiday will do us both the world of good." Jonty was sitting in his chair in the Senior Common Room of St. Bride's College discussing the long vacation and plans he had for it. These, naturally, involved Orlando, who in the past had usually holidayed by visiting other seats of learning, with the occasional dutiful visit to his grandmother in Kent interspersed among the academic outings.

Orlando had no concept of just going off to some place of leisure and relaxing, frittering the time away on walks or sightseeing or bathing. His eyes widened as his friend recounted the sort of things *he'd* got up to in the past—the Riviera, visiting archaeological sites, cruising in the Mediterranean. This seemed to be yet another alien world the sophisticated Jonty was introducing to his naïve friend. When he suggested they should go somewhere *together*, Orlando was appalled.

"Consider it, Dr. Coppersmith, the world is our oyster. Now, before you begin to quibble about the costs, I would remind you my grandmother left her favourite grandson extremely well off, so money is no object. Name where you would like to go and we'll organise it. Shall it be Monte Carlo or the rose red city of Petra?" A glorious smile lit Jonty's face as he made the suggestion, brightening the Stygian gloom which usually infested the room.

"Must we go anywhere, Dr. Stewart?" Orlando was quite content here in his own college among the places and things he knew well. No further unrest had come to St. Bride's since the murders of the previous winter, allowing his love affair with Jonty to blossom as beautifully as the magnolia trees gracing the Fellows' Garden. In his eyes, life was perfect here and now, so why should he go off searching for anything else?

Jonty narrowed his eyes. "Of course we must. I have no intention of spending my long vac festering here. If you won't go with me, I'll go alone." He sniffed. "Though I have gone alone on holiday too often in the past. I was hoping so much that you would see fit to coming with me, so we could share the excitement. Think of the novelty, the exotic food, the flora and fauna that East Anglia can only dream of. Strange languages. Mysterious sights."

It was the novelty Orlando couldn't stop thinking of, or so he told his friend. He'd encountered quite a lot of new things these last few months, particularly when he and Jonty were first acquainted. Now he was hoping for a period of relative calm before the new academic year ensued. The minute he looked into Jonty's eyes, he knew he was beaten—the man was desperate for this break, the chance of a trip with his lover at his side. Who was Orlando to deny him it?

They eventually reached a compromise—three weeks' leave, travelling no further than the Channel Islands. Jonty would find them some nice establishment on Jersey and book tickets for the ferry from Southampton. It would be adventurous, although not too much so; the food would be English (with perhaps a little native cuisine included) and there would be no language barrier. Orlando was particularly pleased about that, as modern languages were not his forte—moreover, as he admitted, the thought of being around exotic foreign ladies terrified him.

For the next week Jonty beavered away with the *Red Guide*, simultaneously picking his mother's brains about hotels, the Honourable Mrs. Stewart being a great source of information about many things, until finally settling for the Beaulieu at St. Aubin.

"It boasts *Three acres of terraced gardens with lawns, Private Tennis Courts, Fishing, and Bathing from the Hotel*," he gleefully explained to Orlando, waving the brochure about. "There are private bathrooms, so you won't risk ladies walking in on you should you forget to shoot the bolt. The additional cost for that will only be sixpence per night, so you won't be risking bankrupting me. Convenient for the train, too."

"It sounds delightful, Jonty," Orlando said, with *liar* written plain on his face. "You should book it."

"Already done. They alleged they were fully booked, August being high season, until they found themselves up against Mama. She spoke to the manager, the owners, probably to King Edward himself—she's wangled us the best two-bedroom suite in the house. I never really appreciated how wonderful it is to have quite such a formidable mother until now..."

📖

"Do you still want 'Jerusalem' sung at your funeral, Dr. Coppersmith?" Jonty began to gently rub his friend's back as the poor man clung to the ship's rail, green to the gills as though desperately trying to fathom out whether he would feel better if he were sick again or not.

"I no longer care, Dr. Stewart. I think I would prefer to die with the minimum of fuss, plus the maximum of expediency. I have enjoyed these last ten months, though I'm greatly afraid I won't survive the journey." Orlando finished his speech with dignity, then sped off to the toilet again.

Jonty looked out at the sea and tried not to think of what would be going on in the gentlemen's conveniences. He felt more than a bit guilty about bringing Orlando on this trip, but how was he to have any idea that his lover would suffer quite so much from seasickness? Orlando hadn't even known it himself, having been on nothing more adventurous than the paddle steamer out of Ramsgate.

There were at least two hours of the voyage left before they could feel decent, solid ground under their feet, then there was the awful prospect of having to do the journey all over again, back to Southampton, in a fortnight's time.

The nightmare of the crossing eventually ended, all the passengers reaching terra firma with much thanks. Orlando swore, afterwards, he'd felt tempted to kneel down and kiss the solid earth beneath his feet at the quay. Plenty of carriages were waiting for custom, so they were soon riding around the wide bay to St. Aubin, able at last to admire the innocuous-looking waters which had managed to wreak such havoc on a delicate digestive tract.

Orlando was recovered enough to smile when he saw their hotel. It was everything the rather overblown brochure had promised and more besides. Their bags were whisked away with just the right amount of efficient deference, the reception clerk was welcoming without being unctuous. Even the suite, once Orlando was entirely convinced it was quite normal for friends of the same sex to take sets of rooms together, was pronounced to be above reproach.

They hadn't long begun to unpack before Jonty suggested it was time to find a small sherry or some such before dinner. He assured his friend it would be the right medicine to enable him to recover his appetite enough to tackle at least some of the delights that they'd spied on the hotel menu.

Orlando was rather affronted, wanting everything to have found its proper place in the suite before they ventured out, but

Jonty insisted, so he struck his colours. Orlando changed into his dinner jacket, newly purchased on his lover's orders as the old one looked more suited to the stalls at the music hall. Properly attired, they went down to the bar.

📖

The dining room was full, mainly married couples of various ages, from the bashful newlyweds who sat in the corner blushing at every remark made to them to the elderly couple—all wrinkles and bright smiles—who sat at a table directly opposite the two Cambridge fellows. This couple, the Tattersalls, had taken a great shine to the two young men as they'd chatted with them over pre-dinner drinks, insisting they reminded them of their sons at a similar age. They seemed won over by Jonty's smile, his obvious good breeding, and Orlando's gravity and beautiful manners.

There were some families at dinner—two had brought their grownup daughters with them. Both girls were plain and seemed rather smitten with the two young men, if blushes or girlish sighs were anything to go by. The only other unmarried couple present was a man perhaps three or four years older than Jonty, accompanied by what could only have been his father, given the strong family resemblance. The younger was a handsome chap whose dark curly hair framed deep blue eyes.

Not that the two fellows of St. Bride's had eyes for anyone else, but one couldn't help noticing these things. They also couldn't help noticing the palpable tension between the two men, shown in their strained politeness and inability to maintain eye contact with each other.

After dinner Jonty and Orlando made up a four for bridge in the sun lounge with the Tattersalls. They proved excellent company, the lady in particular having an impish sense of humour. She chatted away to Jonty, the pair of them giggling

13

like two schoolchildren, despite her being old enough, just, to be his grandmother.

The father and son formed their own bridge four with another married couple, although they were obviously not having half the enjoyment that Orlando and his friend were. Jonty was fascinated, keeping a surreptitious eye on them all evening.

📖

When they got back to their room, Jonty had clearly decided it was character analysis time, despite the fact that Orlando was struggling to arrange, into some sort of acceptable order, the mass of items his friend had strewn everywhere in an attempt to unpack. "That young man's not happy to be here, Orlando. I think his father has made him come, while he'd rather be at home with his sweetheart, not entertaining a surly old curmudgeon."

"I hope you don't feel like you've been dragged along to entertain a surly young curmudgeon." Orlando grinned. "Anyway, it's nothing to do with us." He picked up the tie he'd worn for the journey, finding somewhere to put it carefully away.

"Aren't you even a little bit curious? This is such an opportunity to meet new people, the sort of folk we might never meet at college. Like that delightful old couple—she certainly had the measure even of you at cards, Dr. Coppersmith." Jonty yawned, stretching like a great ginger cat. "This is going to be such a delightful holiday. The hotel is perfect, the food is excellent, I have great hopes for the company and you look less green than you did this morning. Such a lovely colour in your cheeks now." He drew his hand down his lover's face, across his lips. It was the first time they'd touched with any degree of intimacy since they'd left St. Bride's. The caress made Orlando shudder afresh, as if they were touching for the first time. "We may have two bedrooms, but do we really need to use them both? It'd be easy enough to slip across before the early morning tea arrives, if we set your alarm clock."

Orlando looked up, determined to refuse. He was still feeling skittish about staying in a suite of rooms with his lover. Sharing a bed was beyond any imagining although, ironically, the item in question was a glorious double bed such as he'd dreamed, on many an occasion, of sleeping in with Jonty. "I'm not sure I feel sufficiently recovered from the journey to want to do anything *except* sleep." He studied his hands, the shirt he was trying to hang up, anything but his lover.

"That would be fine. I'm as happy to simply slumber next to you as anything else. There are plenty of other days for romance—we could just be fond friends tonight, or pretend to be that old couple we played cards with. Still very much in love yet beyond the thralls of passion." Jonty gently touched his friend's hand.

Orlando felt as if a spider was crawling down the back of his neck, and his discomfiture must have been plain. "What if we slept apart, just for tonight?"

They had reached the crux of why he'd been so keen not to come on holiday. He was frightened of taking their relationship outside the college walls, displaying it to the world. Within the ivy-clad, male-dominated locality of St. Bride's, it had been easy to maintain a friendship which was more than close without raising a suspicious eyebrow. He'd spent little time with Jonty out of Cambridge, apart from a visit or two to London, where they'd stayed in the relatively safe environs of the Stewart family home. To be with the man in a strange place was to put himself at risk of making a demonstration of his affection by an unguarded look or touch.

Any footman could walk through the streets of town in his bowler-hatted Sunday best, hand in hand with a parlour maid.

A pair of dons could never be allowed such freedom; not in Cambridge and certainly not on Jersey. If they ever were mad enough to be tempted, all they had to do was remember the law—two years of hard labour and public disgrace would be no holiday.

Jonty slammed down the toothbrush he'd been unpacking. "Oh, go and sleep in the bath if you want to! I haven't the heart to put up with this nonsense. I'm going to sleep in my own bed, in my own soft pyjamas, with my own book. If you change your mind and decide to join me, make sure you knock, because I might just have found other company." He spun on his heels, entering his bedroom with a slam of the door which caused the windows to shake.

Orlando contemplated opening the door again to give his friend a piece of his mind, but didn't want to end up in a full-blown row in a public building. He also contemplated going in and giving Jonty the most comprehensive kissing he'd ever received. He decided against that, as it was probably exactly what the little swine wanted, so must be avoided at all costs. Even at the cost of a miserable night alone.

Eventually, after tidying everything to his own immaculate standards, he trudged his weary way into his bedroom and readied himself for sleep.

At two o'clock in the morning the heavens opened, torrential rain driving against the windowpanes while thunder pealed as loud as cannon fire. Orlando leapt out of bed without a second thought, making his way through their little sitting room into Jonty's bedroom. He didn't knock, knowing by now that any threats from his friend about *finding company* were all bluster, to find him standing by the window, shivering.

"Come on, Jonty—you'll get cold, you know." Orlando put his arms around the man's shoulders, which felt icy through his silken pyjama jacket. Jonty both hated thunderstorms and was fascinated by them. Orlando had often found him looking

16

out of the window of his room at St. Bride's while the lightning rent the sky, making the college's very foundations seem to shake. He could go into an almost dreamlike state, distracted and seemingly unaware of his surroundings, having to be coaxed back gently into the real world. Orlando wondered whether some of the awful things which had happened to Jonty at school had taken place during storms, although he'd never been brave enough to ask.

Orlando took his lover to bed, tenderly soothing him back to sleep, holding tight as each new clap of thunder brought a shuddering through Jonty's frame. Eventually the storm passed eastwards and they could both fall asleep, Jonty as content as a child in his mother's arms. Orlando felt masterful, protective and very much in love. If anyone walked in, he had a legitimate medical excuse to be present. Or so he assured himself.

📖

Thanks to Orlando's innate body clock, the chambermaid delivering the early morning tea found the two men in their own separate beds, above reproach.

Jonty soon brought his cup into the other room and snuggled under the sheet, the night having been too muggy to need blankets. "Will you wear that tie today, the one I bought you at Easter? The ladies would be very impressed."

Only a snort came in reply. "Most of the ladies I meet seem impressed at anything."

"Do you meet very many ladies? Seems you're living a double life, then, because I never see you talking to them."

Orlando thumped Jonty around the back of the head with his pillow. "Imbecile. Well, I'm going to take advantage of the 'private bathroom at sixpence a night extra' to prepare myself for the day. You can shave at the basin while I'm in the tub."

Tea shot out of Jonty's nose, making him splutter in an undignified manner. The thought of Orlando issuing an invitation to be viewed in the bath—such a thing hadn't happened since the afternoon the man had got drunk at St. Thomas's college, not even when they'd shared a bathroom while staying at the Stewart family home. It seemed marvellously out of character.

"I'll certainly take up the offer or we'll never see breakfast. I can smell the bacon already, although that might just be an olfactory illusion. Breakfast, then church—I saw you wince, but we *are* going—then off to the beach." Jonty squeezed his lover's thigh. "I saw you wince when I mentioned *beach* as well, so you'll just have to apply your stiff upper lip."

📖

Jonty sat down on a rock to get on with removing his shoes and socks.

"What are you doing?"

"Going paddling, Orlando." The holiday air had affected them both, so using Christian names now seemed acceptable, even outside their suite. Jonty suddenly looked up at the awkward figure which towered over him. "Oh, Orlando. You'd never been in the Bishop's Cope, you'd never been punting—please, *please* don't tell me that you have never paddled."

"I have actually paddled on a number of occasions, when I was taken to see my grandmother in Kent." Orlando attempted to look a man at once dignified and completely *au fait* with the delights of the seaside.

Jonty assumed a sly look. "When exactly was the last time you indulged in this wild activity?"

Orlando mumbled, "When I was seven."

Jonty giggled. "Then you had better ruddy well get your

socks off and your trouser bottoms rolled up, because you're coming with me."

Orlando felt distinctly miffed. He contemplated refusing to do any such thing, but decided to obey orders, stuffing his socks into the toes of his shoes, then tying the laces together in imitation of his lover. The reason for this strange procedure became obvious when Jonty slung his shoes around his neck, leaving his hands free to continue picking up stones for skimming or shells for stuffing in his pockets.

As he watched Jonty turning over rocks to search for tiny crustaceans which he then let run over his palms, it struck Orlando more than ever that at heart his friend was just an overgrown boy. An enormous crab got rooted out, a good three inches across the carapace, which Jonty expertly picked up to wave at his friend.

"What a whopper—look!" He passed the creature over, grinning as Orlando inevitably grabbed it the wrong way, earning a sharp nip on his fingers.

He flung the offending animal away, shaking his sore hand and cursing like a sailor.

"Such language!" Jonty hooted with laughter. "Look, take him *across* the back, so all your fingers are out of his reach." He demonstrated the technique, then made his friend do the same.

Orlando took up the vicious creature, more gingerly than if it had been a bomb, breaking into a smile of delight when the method worked. "He's a beauty. Not big enough for tea, though." Laughing, he placed the crab down among the rocks, returning to follow his friend.

The tide was ebbing, revealing rock pools full of shrimps which Jonty caught in his hand, then let spring out of his grasp with a giggle. Orlando soon learned that game too, proving much more adept at catching the little invertebrates and the darting fishes than his lover. It was like being a child again, except there hadn't been that much room for play in his childhood, so there was time to be caught up. Yet again, he could experience a freedom with Jonty that he'd never known before they met.

Jonty picked up a huge ormer shell, holding it to the light so that they could both admire the mother-of-pearl glittering in the sunlight.

"Beautiful. Eh?"

"Indeed." Although Orlando didn't mean the shell so much as the man holding it.

Tired, eventually, of annoying the occupants of the rock pools, they walked along the waterline, the warm sea just lapping over their feet. The occasional wave came in with slightly more force, making them jump out of the way, splashing and laughing.

It took a whole mile of wandering for Jonty to begin to make mischief, starting to splash just a little too deliberately in a particular direction. Orlando didn't notice at first, blaming the splatters on his trousers on the swell. When he did realise what was going on, he handled the situation admirably, deciding that revenge is a dish best eaten cold. While he would have loved to dunk Jonty head to foot, there and then, more pleasure was to be had by quietly removing himself from flying water range before making his plans.

Seaweed wasn't the most pleasant thing to handle straight from the sea. Jonty usually found it disagreeable on the feet when he had to wade through it, but it was truly disgusting when someone forcibly stuffed it down the back of his trousers. Orlando had executed his vengeance.

"You swine!"

"You're no longer dealing with some naïve young man who's spent all his days in a haze of academia. I'm learning, so you'd better watch your step." Orlando looked smug, strikingly handsome in his triumph.

Jonty fished down his pants to extract the offending piece of algae. He flung it at his friend, missed by a mile, then laughed. "I've only ever wanted you to be my equal, Orlando. I'm looking forward enormously to the day when you tease me both mercilessly and with aplomb." He reached out his hand to take his lover's, remembered they were in public, shrugged in apology and walked on.

They strolled the length of the beach till Jonty's pockets were so full of shells he'd begun to rattle. Drying off their feet on their handkerchiefs proved largely ineffective, as did hopping madly about so that the clean, dry foot couldn't be infected with sand before it made its way into its sock. Sand always found its way into every available crevice and was bound to begin to creep into their shoes, regardless, before they were halfway off the beach. The long walk back to Corbière station would be uncomfortable, although it wouldn't spoil the delights of the previous hours.

Jonty felt the glow which always came with having enlightened his friend, introducing some new pleasure—innocent or not—into the man's life. Orlando had shown a spark of delight in having effectively taken a rare revenge and Jonty wondered whether he was plotting other ways of getting one over on him. *This holiday is showing every sign of being more than enjoyable.*

On the station platform they saw the young man from the hotel looking much happier without his usual companion. He acknowledged them with a tilt of the head, which was all the encouragement Jonty needed to effect an introduction. "I believe you're staying at the Beaulieu, as we are? My name is Stewart. This is my friend Coppersmith." Jonty waved his hand to indicate Orlando, who had yet to venture any closer.

"They call me Ainslie, sir. Matthew Ainslie. I'm delighted to meet you." The man held out his hand, producing an engaging smile in the process.

"Have you been on Jersey long, Mr. Ainslie?"

"Matthew, I insist you call me Matthew." He smiled again. "I...*we* arrived three days ago. My father and I always come to one of the Channel Islands once a year—he feels the air agrees with him."

"I hope it will agree with us, too. It's our first time here and I've been very pleasantly surprised so far. I dare say we'll be picking your brains about the best places to visit."

"Your friend over there is enjoying himself, too?" Ainslie indicated Orlando, who looked nothing like a man enjoying himself.

A man trying to win the most surly face competition, perhaps. "I believe he is, although he doesn't often show it. He enjoyed playing bridge last night with the Tattersalls. Such a delightful couple."

Ainslie smiled. "They beat us soundly on Friday night. I wouldn't like to meet Mrs. Tattersall in a rubber if high stakes were in order, although she could charm the birds out of the trees." His face suddenly changed. "Please excuse me. I can see my father—he'll want me to attend him." A smile and the man was gone, leaving Jonty's interest more piqued than ever.

After another excellent dinner, the fours for bridge were different from Saturday evening. The Ainslies played against Mrs. Tattersall, who was paired with Orlando, Jonty and Mr. Tattersall having opted to observe the fun. The Tattersall-Coppersmith pair trounced the opposition, even when they were obviously not trying, which made it ten times worse. The elder Ainslie's temper was beginning to fray as rubber after rubber went down, until he snapped at his son, on whom no blame could be fairly laid. Matthew was a far more competent player than his father.

For Jonty the fascination lay not with the play (that was a foregone conclusion) but in what the eyes around the table were doing. Orlando watched Ainslie's hands in fascination as he skidded the cards over the table. This man was a talented shuffler and dealer, the sort who would be interesting to see playing alongside a competent partner. While Orlando watched Ainslie's hands, the man watched his. Orlando had long, delicate fingers, fingers with which Jonty was intimately acquainted, which he found both beautiful and capable of causing havoc in the bedroom. Ainslie followed the graceful movements his partner's digits made as they picked up and sorted his hand, caressing the backs of the cards.

Jonty observed the way that Ainslie was watching. He would not forget it.

Chapter Two

"Jonty, wake up. It's time you were back to your own bed." Orlando gently nudged his friend, nudges that became rougher as the sleeper refused to respond.

"Go back to my bed yourself, Orlando. The chambermaid won't remember who slept where the night before this one."

"She will, I know she will. Please, for my sake. I can hear people stirring already."

Jonty had to admit defeat, now that Orlando was developing a stubborn streak. Anyway, he was jolly grateful to have a wangled a night in his lover's bed to start with. His strategy had been beautifully simple; he'd come up to the suite well before the game of cards had ended, so that when his companion himself retired for the night, it was to find his bed warm, welcoming and full of a silk-pyjama-clad Jonty. He knew Orlando wouldn't have the heart to boot him out. Jonty had come on holiday with several aims in mind, one of which was to get his friend into a nice double bed, rather than the cramped conditions of a standard St. Bride's single.

Jonty felt this was a small triumph. When they spent a week with the Stewarts during the Easter break, it had taken Orlando four days to give his lover even the tiniest of goodnight kisses by the bedroom door. That was after checking one hundred times that the coast was clear. The fifth night had, however, only required two dozen glances around before a rather more exciting kiss was delivered. The sixth night a whole series of kisses had led them inside Jonty's room, although the bed had never been reached.

He inwardly chuckled at the recollection of that week, especially at Orlando and Helena Stewart meeting for the first time. Papa had been easy, shaking his guest's hand heartily, then immediately launching into a discussion about bridge and the best methods of bidding. Orlando had been put at as near his ease as he was going to be on strange territory, although when mother had steamed into the room, full of apologies for her having been held up at a meeting, then disapprobation for her son for having had the cheek to turn up early, the shy young man had frozen entirely.

Jonty had often compared his mama to HMS *Dreadnought*. Orlando had been shocked to hear such filial disloyalty, but "*Dreadnought*" didn't cover the half of it. She was a large woman, it was true, although she must have been a beauty in her prime, and her personality was immense. Formidable did not in any way do her justice. Orlando had just about managed a bow with his handshake then had watched in amusement as Jonty was, in no particular order, hugged fiercely, upbraided for being so thin, pinched on the cheek, made to sit down and forced to eat cake.

"What are you grinning about, pest?" Orlando swatted his backside, bringing Jonty back to the present. "No, don't tell me now, come back when your tea's here."

Jonty reappeared ten minutes later, having been found by the chambermaid looking as if he'd been in his bed all night. "I was thinking about when you first met Mama. You could hardly say more than *yes* or *no* to her."

"I was observing her for tips I could use to rein you in. Any person who could reduce you to silence *and* make you do what you're told must be pretty special." He drew Jonty's hand to his lips for a brief contact. "Do you know, when she smiled my

25

heart melted. She turned into your image, and at last I knew where you got your inner strength from."

"Well, Mama was exceedingly impressed with you, too." Jonty broke into an uncanny impression of his mother. "Such beautiful manners dear, so obviously well brought up. I did wonder if he was connected to the Glamorgan Coppersmiths but it appears not. I am so pleased that you brought him to stay. I like him very much, even though he needs a good feed— preferably several. I shall enjoy his company any time that you would wish to bring him home."

As they laughed, Jonty's hopes were raised that his friend was going to begin to relax. He knew how much Orlando worried about being seen in public, that in his mind love was for behind the closed doors of one of two sets of rooms at St. Bride's. It had been agony getting him to accept that the Stewarts' London home might be an acceptable place for it, too.

Another aim of this holiday was to get Orlando to unwind so, with this in mind, Jonty began his next piece of carefully planned strategy. "Now, is it the old Blues' blazers today, then?"

The contrast of dark and light sportsmen's blazers made a big hit with all the ladies in the restaurant. There were several murmurs of unrest from said ladies' husbands as they tried to wrest their spouses' attention back to themselves. The two spinsters looked as if they might just swoon. The two young fellows of St. Bride's ignored all the female glances, ate heartily, drank two pots of coffee, then returned to their room to add the finishing touches to their appearance before setting off for the day.

📖

Matthew stood on the terrace, enjoying a cigarette. The appearance at the Beaulieu of two agreeable young men, both of whom could play cards well, had brightened his holiday. It wasn't the most exciting way to spend a vacation, pandering to a demanding relative, so any distraction would prove enjoyable. Particularly a distraction as attractive as Coppersmith. He'd been thinking on the man since last evening—the depths of his dark eyes, the curl of his lashes. There'd been every indication, in their conversation, that he might even share some of Matthew's particular interests, which made the brown eyes even more alluring.

As Dr. Stewart and Dr. Coppersmith emerged from the hotel, Matthew approached them, smiling. "Lovely day, gentlemen. What are your plans?" He looked from the dark man to the fair one, then back again, waiting for Dr. Coppersmith to answer.

Eventually, after a pause just the right side of discourtesy, he piped up. "Dr. Stewart has suggested a walk around the bay to St. Helier, then a visit to the market."

This would be no great distance; there would be plenty of time for other, more athletic pursuits. "Perhaps you would be free for a game of tennis this afternoon?" Matthew directed his offer firmly at Dr. Coppersmith. Dr. Stewart was pleasant enough, but he wasn't Matthew's type. Not by any definition of the word.

"I would be delighted, if that's acceptable to you, Dr. Stewart?" Dr. Coppersmith turned to Dr. Stewart, as if unwilling to agree anything without his friend's assent.

"I have a new book to read, Dr. Coppersmith, and I'd welcome some time to do so." Dr. Stewart cast a sideways glance at Matthew, who hoped the man wouldn't notice any relief or anticipation displayed on his face. Dr. Stewart seemed a very shrewd customer, the sort who might look into your eyes and see your soul. Matthew kept his gaze fixed on Orlando.

"Shall we say three o'clock then?" Matthew paused for the nod of assent. "Very good, I'll book the courts and hire some rackets." He cast his cigarette butt into the flowerbed and went back inside to find his father, who'd no doubt tell him off for being away so long.

"Matthew. A word." Mr. Ainslie spoke sternly, as he always seemed to do these days. His son followed him through the hallway, then into the gardens until they found a quiet spot overlooking the long, curving bay. "What are your plans for the day?"

"Nothing special. I have a game of tennis arranged for this afternoon." Matthew tried to sound casual, hiding any tinge of excitement he felt.

"Tennis?" His father sniffed.

There was a wealth of meaning in the sound, as if Mr. Ainslie knew well enough what his son had in mind. Perhaps he did; he'd made that much plain these last few weeks.

"Yes, with Dr. Coppersmith."

"You, sir, would be better employed playing tennis with one of the young ladies. You know my feelings on the matter and there's a limit to my patience. Most men of your age are married, settling down to have a family. Don't you want our business to be handed down, as I've handed it to you?"

Matthew didn't reply, resisting any temptation to point out that his father had little option regarding handing over duties within the company. They'd had this argument, the great marriage debate, innumerable times and the result was always the same. His nature to be sacrificed on the altar of the Ainslie name, whatever that was worth.

"I'll take your silence as assent, then." Ainslie senior gestured towards the path, a gravel track which led up to the tennis courts, then beyond to a small copse. "Play your game, if you must, but that's the end to it. No more of your nonsense." He strode away, leaving Matthew wondering how his life could have become so bloody complicated.

Orlando and Jonty strolled leisurely down to the gate, coming out on the road to the quay. Orlando broke the comfortable silence which had settled between them. "He seems a pleasant chap, that Ainslie."

Jonty giggled. "I would say that you've got yourself an admirer there, Dr. Coppersmith."

Orlando stopped dead in his tracks. "I beg your pardon?"

"An admirer. A devotee. A follower." Jonty spoke in his best talking-to-my-four-year-old nephew tone.

"Oh, I understand the word, I just don't see what you're getting at." It was true. He'd never considered that Matthew might be any more than a rather lonely chap seeking the company of people his own age. "Why should you think he admires me?" They leaned against the harbour rail.

"He couldn't take his eyes off you last night, not over dinner, not over bridge. Seemed to be fascinated with your hands, by which I don't mean your cards. I wonder what transpired over that table after I went to my unsullied bed?"

"Seem to remember it was *my* bed," Orlando murmured. He carried on aloud. "After bridge we took a brandy together then chatted. His father owns a publishing house in the city and Mr. Ainslie is one of the directors. We had a very interesting conversation about the works of Oscar Wilde, although I had to profess ignorance of them."

Jonty giggled again. "I should think so, too!" He stopped laughing, an unusually serious look on his face. "Did he say anything specific about Oscar Wilde or his works?"

Orlando considered. "I don't think I really understood a lot of what he said. I was very tired, you know, just trying to be polite, nodding or shaking my head in what I hoped were the right places."

Jonty sighed. "Well I hope it turns out all right, Orlando, but do be careful, please."

Orlando still had no idea what he was being warned about, and didn't want to show his ignorance, so they resumed their walk. A stroll around the quay led them down to the beach, where the tide had ebbed enough to leave a clear line of hard sand, widening every moment, suitable for walking along to the island's little capital.

They hardly spoke except to point out the two fine forts which guarded each side of the bay, Orlando muttering fevered calculations about trajectories in an attempt to work out whether they could cover the entire sweep with their guns. The sun beat down into their faces, making hard work of things, to the extent that they had to take off their jackets and ties then loosen their collars. This made Orlando feel like he was some corner boy, although Jonty reassured him it would be acceptable on the beach.

"Might even get you into the sea one of these days." Jonty waved airily at the ocean.

They'd each bought magnificent new bathing costumes, blue and white striped and just short enough to show off their manly calves. Orlando was dreading having to appear in them in public. Perhaps he would be lucky—rain for the whole fortnight—although the barometer in the hotel kept promising fair weather. At least he'd been spared bathing for this day and Jonty conceded that they'd best make themselves respectable again when they reached St. Helier.

They wandered the little streets of the town, noting many places which they might like to come back to explore. They wandered past the Corn Exchange, finding a small café where they could take a well-earned, cool glass of lemonade and watch the world go by. Nursemaids with babies in perambulators, little boys carrying kites to the park, and ladies in their finest summer outfits passed by, the ladies then re-passing in case they'd not been sufficiently noticed the first time. The two men commented on some of the people but as often as not they were silent, simply content, supremely confident in their friendship.

In time they wandered on, poking their noses into any shops which took their fancy, especially the one where Orlando could top up his dwindling toffee supply. Eventually they reached the indoor market, where the sights and smells created a unique, evocative mixture. From one of the stalls the overwhelming scent of freesias took their breath away. Orlando had never smelt the like before; he insisted on buying a huge bunch to take back to their suite, then kept placing his nose inside the paper to take great inhalations of the flowers' sweet perfume. He was terribly tempted by the jewel-like strawberries, too, although Jonty insisted they would spoil his lunch. Instead, he dragged Orlando off into a little second-hand bookshop where they rummaged happily among the dusty tomes, until Jonty declared he was so starving they should take something to eat.

"For lunch, Orlando, we'll have a gastronomic treat such as is rarely exceeded anywhere. Wait here by the fountain and don't annoy the fish." Jonty scuttled away until his dark blond head was soon lost among the crowds.

When he did reappear, he beckoned Orlando to follow him off into a corner of the marketplace, where he was leaning on a stall, passing money over the counter to receive two paper bundles in return. Jonty handed one to his friend and grinned.

Orlando peered inside the wrappings. Notwithstanding the glorious smell which emerged from them, he was extremely wary of the contents. "This is what you've made such a fuss about?"

"Fish and chips at their very best. Observe the golden batter, take in the wonderful aroma. Add a little salt or vinegar too, should you desire, then just indulge."

31

Orlando was quite ready to indulge although he couldn't work out the procedure. The Bishop's Cope had been shock enough to his system, but there at least they had plates and cutlery, not food served in newspapers (disreputable ones at that). Here there wasn't a fork in sight.

"Use your fingers, man. God gave us those before he gave us forks, you know." Jonty picked up the biggest chip he could find and stuck it whole into his mouth, huffing at how hot it was. "Oh, these are absolutely beautiful. I've eaten caviar, French truffles, the finest Belgian chocolate, yet this culinary treat is beyond them all." He stopped abruptly, seeing that Orlando hadn't even attempted his food. "What *is* the problem?"

"My hands will get all greasy and covered in salt."

"Then lick your fingers afterwards. Or I could lick them for you, if you wish." He cocked his head to one side. "Only don't put vinegar on them if that's your intention, I just like salt."

Orlando liberally doused his portion with both salt *and* vinegar, gave Jonty a look of triumph, then set to demolishing the lot. He even licked his fingers afterwards, feeling only slightly guilty about the shame it would have brought his mother to have seen him do it. Never mind that his mother would never have let him indulge in Liquorice Allsorts, either, and if she knew what he'd been up to at St. Bride's with Dr. Stewart, she would be turning in her grave.

They strolled leisurely, extremely leisurely, there having been plenty of food in those newspapers, back to the railway station, where they rested peacefully in the shade until the train arrived to take them back to St. Aubin.

As they journeyed around the bay again, Orlando leaned over to Jonty and simply said, "Glad you persuaded me to come on holiday. Best thing I've done for ages. Thank you."

Sixteen little words which knocked any sensible reply out of his friend.

Jonty was lying on the settee in the sitting room of their suite, reading glasses perched on his nose. He had a bottle of lemonade, a packet of peppermint creams and a Conan Doyle. No distractions, though, Orlando having gone off to play tennis with Matthew Ainslie. A glorious hour or two were in prospect.

Or they were until the door burst open, a racket went flying through the air, just missing his feet, and a very cross man in white flannels announced, "Ainslie tried to kiss me!"

"Well, of course he did." Jonty didn't spill even one drop of his lemonade. "I told you it was in the air yet you didn't take the slightest notice. Serves you right." He tried very hard not to look up from his book, despite the long streak of fury which was buzzing around near him.

"We didn't even get to the tennis courts." Orlando paced from the door to the window then back again. "He took me up into the grove of trees at the back of the garden, 'to see the honey buzzards,' he said. Honey buzzards my elbow!" Orlando stopped in front of him, wrenched the book from his hand and flung it in the direction of the racket. "Then you have the audacity to say 'serves you right'."

Jonty looked up this time to find that Orlando wasn't just angry. His face was suffused with fear, a fear Jonty hadn't seen there since the dreadful time of the St. Bride's murders. "Sit down." He reached out for his friend's hand, drawing him to sit beside him. "Tell me exactly what happened."

He stroked the hand tenderly, trying to give every reassurance through his touches. Orlando must have been frightened stiff to have been accosted, but the man had to learn that the world wasn't full of academics whose thoughts were always in their theorems and never in their trousers.

"We went into the thicket a little way before we stopped. I thought he was going to show me a nest or something, only he took my arm and turned me round to face him. Before I knew what was going on, he stuck his face into mine then tried to kiss me. On the lips..." Orlando looked scandalised.

The offended expression made Jonty giggle, quite inappropriately. "Did your mother never tell you not to go into the woods with strange men?"

"I'm glad you find it so very amusing. I understand that I'm a constant source of merriment to you, but I'd hoped that you'd have been sympathetic." Orlando rose and stormed into his bedroom with such a slam of the door that Jonty feared for the hinges.

He sighed, mentally kicking himself. *When will you ever learn to hold your tongue? He's frightened and confused. You know he's petrified enough of touching you in public, of giving himself away. How must he have felt with a stranger?* He rose then gently knocked on the door.

"Go away, Dr. Stewart."

Jonty opened the door a few inches. A pillow came flying through the air, glancing off his head. It was obviously a throwing day *chez* Coppersmith.

Jonty took his handkerchief from his pocket to wave it dramatically. "Truce, Orlando?"

"Bugger off, Jonty."

He ignored the remark, coming over and sitting down on the bed next to his friend. "Big idiot's come to say he's sorry. Doesn't expect to be forgiven but wants to listen, properly this time." He smiled tenderly, then stretched out along the bed, parallel with Orlando although not touching, making a nice geometrical shape with the wooden headboard, which his favourite mathematician would have probably appreciated at another time. Now, no doubt, he was trying to overcome the desire to thump his friend.

"Why do you want to hear? So you can laugh at my innocence again?" Orlando huffed, crossing his arms.

"I want to hear because I want to understand. What did you do when Ainslie pushed his face in yours, which is probably a very good description of what happened. I can imagine it exactly." Jonty ventured a tiny smile.

"I slapped his face." Orlando screwed his eyes, his cheeks bright red. "I told him that I had no intention of kissing him, then or at any point in the future. Then he apologised and said he'd misunderstood, though what there was to understand is beyond me, so I came back here." He opened his eyes to look pleadingly at Jonty, the anger in his eyes gone even if the fear was still in situ. "I want to go home. Back to St. Bride's."

"Oh, we can't, Orlando." Jonty was crestfallen. "We need this holiday. I need this holiday. I know that you're not going to want to face this man again, but you're just going to have to find the courage. He probably won't bother you a second time, not after you made your feelings so plain. Slapped his face?" He ventured a hand over to his friend's arm and gently tapped it. "Good for you."

Orlando turned to face him. "Did I do right, Jonty? I had no idea, truly. I thought that you were overreacting with that 'he looked at your hands all night' remark. I don't want to kiss anyone except you. You know that, don't you?"

"Well, of course I do. Known that for a long time. Look, Matthew Ainslie won't be the last to try it on, you must realise that. You've a handsome face and a winning smile, when you care to use it. That air of aloofness would drive many an admirer wild." Jonty caressed the face he loved so much, savouring—as he did every time—the contrast of rough with smooth textures. "You've never realised, sitting in the little world of Bride's, that you're an exceedingly attractive man. People you talk to are going to take notice."

"But you talk to any and everyone, Jonty, flirt with them too. What do you do if they respond?" Orlando drew his lover's hand to his chest, letting it rest over his heart. It was a habitual gesture, one they both cherished.

"Run like stink in the other direction, generally. Plead that my heart belongs to my college and no other. I had to lie once— said I belonged to an evangelical sect which insisted on a vow of chastity, although that was with a particularly persistent lady. Never had to resort to a slap, however I'll bear it in mind for extreme occasions."

Orlando leaned up on his elbow. "Did your mother tell *you* not to go into the woods with strange men? Or women?"

"As hard as you may find it to believe, my mother and father gave me no advice about carnal matters. These things are simply not talked about in 'nice' families. The farmer's daughter is better prepared than the gentleman's—she sees the bull taken to the cows or the pigs farrowing. My poor sister had a terrible time on her wedding night. She had no idea whatsoever about the male anatomy or what parts of it were used for. Came straight home to Mama in torrents of tears swearing that her husband was a misshapen, disgusting brute. She had to be told very plainly the truth of things. I did slightly better. Father warned me, when I was sixteen, not to get any girls into trouble. I thought he meant keeping them out late or making them steal things."

"My mother never told me anything, either, more's the pity. She didn't give me any advice about life except that I should find myself a nice, respectable wife and have two nice, respectable children. She never saw fit to inform me how they were to be begot. Father said that if I 'found myself stimulated'—his words, not mine—I should take a cold bath then read *Pilgrim's Progress*." Orlando sighed, lying back again, looking very young and vulnerable in his white flannels with open-necked shirt.

Jonty could understand why Matthew had been so enflamed. He'd felt the same way when he'd first seen Orlando in his cricket whites. There'd been a game for St. Bride's against St. Thomas's college; Orlando had thrown himself about manfully in the field, his lithe body looking so athletic that Jonty had been forced to fan himself. After the game he'd rushed the man straight back to his set—within two minutes of their passing through the door, Orlando's whites had joined Jonty's suit on the floor and his long, delicate fingers were roaming over his lover's body, wreaking havoc. The memory was doing nothing for Jonty's composure, which was fighting a losing battle with excitement.

"Did you ever look for a wife, Orlando?" Jonty tried to keep his mind above waist level. And away from anything male.

"Honest truth, Jonty, I was too scared. Never got on with girls, you know that. My mother invited plenty to tea, although I always found an excuse to be elsewhere or take my leave early. I just thought I was shy, that I'd grow out of it. Never realised why." He drew up Jonty's hand to press it to his lips. "I realise now."

"Do you want *me* to talk to Ainslie? I'll make it plain that if anyone should be going home it's him and that unpleasant father of his, who, I'm fairly certain, was trying to cheat at cards last night, but that's by-the-by. Do you want me to do this for you?"

"Let me think about it, I don't want to make matters worse. Discretion might be the better part of valour this time."

Jonty lazily reached over, began to trace circles on Orlando's shirt. "We have a good hour or so before we have to be getting changed for dinner. Would you be thinking of seducing me now, or are you thrusting me back into the arms of Sherlock Holmes?"

Orlando looked shocked. "I won't be thinking of seducing you at all until we're back in college. At least, if I think of it, I

37

won't be doing anything about it. It's too risky, you know that."

Jonty shrugged. He did know it, or at least Orlando's opinion on the subject. The man had made it plain that he didn't want to put them in any jeopardy while they were away from St. Bride's and that included no indulging in sex.

Or what passed for sex between them as, despite the fact they'd been lovers for months, they'd still not achieved bodily union. Jonty was becoming, if not desperate, then extremely anxious to have a proper consummation. He'd been hoping that the sea air, the wonderfully romantic location and plenty of seafood would loosen Orlando's straitjacket of conservatism. But coming away from his safe haven had made the man even more nervous and reserved. If things carried on the way they were, then even mutual pleasure by hands which stroked or caressed would be impossible this holiday.

"Do I get anything, then? For being a good boy?" Jonty swallowed hard; while he hated to beg, he needed to be shown some sort of physical affection.

"I'll give you what Ainslie wanted—" Orlando laid a tender kiss on his lover's lips, "—although you'll get no more at present." He picked up his own book. "Inspector Bucket and I are off to the bath where I shall soak until I feel clean enough from my encounter in the woods to face the rest of the guests."

"That's the spirit, Orlando." Jonty smiled affectionately, if ruefully, watching as his friend went off to attack the taps. "Though I think Matthew Ainslie wanted a lot more from you than that kiss."

Irrespective of what Matthew may have wanted, neither he nor his father was participating in pre-dinner drinks, nor in the meal itself. Their absence didn't go unnoticed, Jonty remarking quietly, "Perhaps he's too ashamed to come down tonight and face you."

Orlando huffed. "They're probably just taking their meal elsewhere, you'll see."

Nevertheless, something was amiss. An unusually strained atmosphere seemed to pervade the hotel staff, the tension making everyone strangely on edge. Eventually Mrs. Tattersall decided she must venture the questions they were all dying to ask. She called over the manager, Greenwood. "Are Mr. Ainslie and his son not dining with us tonight? Is everything quite well with them?"

The manager lowered his voice, aware that every ear in the restaurant was straining to hear his comments. "I am very much afraid Mr. Ainslie senior was taken ill this afternoon."

"Is there anything we can do to help?" Even if Mrs. Tattersall hadn't shown any affection for the older man, her maternal instinct must have been to lend a hand to his son.

"I regret to say that Mr. Ainslie was pronounced dead by the doctor." Greenwood lowered his voice even further. "He has been taken to the hospital."

"Dear me. Young Mr. Ainslie—is anyone with him?"

"The doctor gave him a sedative, I believe. I hope we'll see him at breakfast tomorrow."

Jonty, shamelessly eavesdropping, laid down his fork, unable to continue eating. "We should go to see him, Orlando." He saw the pained look on his friend's face then rephrased himself. "*I* should go to see him. He shouldn't be left alone at such a time, so far from home."

"You'll go to his aid even after what happened today?" Orlando face couldn't have looked more astonished.

Jonty nodded. "It's only right for someone to do so and it would be better me than you."

Matthew Ainslie sat in the window seat, an unopened packet of medicine, the doctor's prescription, on the table beside him. What a bloody day it had proved to be, from start to bitter end. He'd been such an idiot up in the woods behind the tennis courts, practically throwing himself on someone he hardly knew. Yes, Dr. Coppersmith had looked stunningly attractive in his linen shirt and trousers, a scarf tied artlessly around his neck—Matthew squirmed at the recollection. Why the hell had he plunged in, trusting only to instinct and the answers to questions so casually posed the night before? Were these the actions of a discreet, sensible man?

Obviously not, if the wallop to his face was anything to go by. His cheek still stung, as did his pride, burning with mortification at his own stupidity. Where had his much-vaunted caution been, his insistence on discretion? He supposed he had his reasons, although they sounded pretty thin as his conscience used them to charge him with folly. He was so determined to wrap himself up in thoughts of white flannels and tennis rackets—anything but think about the thing which had really hurt him today—he almost missed the gentle knock on his door.

"Come in. Ah, Dr. Stewart, can I help you?"

"I was wondering whether there was anything I—we—could do for you, Mr. Ainslie? We were so sorry to hear about your father."

Matthew, like many a decent English gentleman, had been brought up not to show emotion even at the most difficult of times. He kept to his training now. "Thank you, Dr. Stewart, but not at present. I've sent notification to our firm, and we've no other close family who need to be informed. I'm just awaiting word from the doctor."

Dr. Stewart raised an eyebrow. "The doctor?"

Matthew took a deep breath, fighting hard to maintain the stiff upper lip which seemed so determined to relax itself. "Yes. Although he can't be sure until the...my father has been fully examined, he believes this may have been murder."

Dr. Stewart started, more than Matthew had expected. "I'm so sorry to hear that. When did it happen?"

"I think it may have been when I was playing tennis with your friend." Matthew tried to control his voice. "I left him, alive, just after we'd had lunch. When I returned here I found..." His fingers writhed around each other.

"Please don't continue, it's upsetting enough for you." Dr. Stewart rose to leave. "Mr. Ainslie, our offer of help is redoubled."

Matthew, knowing they'd another important matter to deal with, raised a hand to stop him. "Would you be so kind as to pass on my apologies to your colleague? We had a...misunderstanding earlier today." He looked Dr. Stewart straight in the eye without flinching, a show of spirit he hoped would impress the younger man.

"Dr. Coppersmith told me exactly what happened." Dr. Stewart's eye shone bright as a tiger's. A tiger protecting its cub.

Matthew considered his words carefully. "Then you may well know that we had a conversation last night after cards. Certain works of Oscar Wilde were discussed. I fear that I misinterpreted some things Dr. Coppersmith said and acted upon them rather precipitately this afternoon." He thought again, uncomfortably, of Dr. Coppersmith saying yes or no in what he'd assumed were the significant places when *Dorian Grey* or *Earnest* were mentioned.

Dr. Stewart bowed, a true gentleman. "I'll pass on your explanation to him. I hope that he'll accept it. Good night." He nodded, turned, and departed, leaving Matthew to wonder if all the mistakes he'd made the last few days could be dealt with so easily.

Chapter Three

The possibility of being in the proximity of a murderer again galvanised Orlando in a quite astonishing manner. Jonty had eventually returned to the bar rather shaken, given his news, then insisted he'd take an early night. He'd anticipated that his friend would make every excuse not to share a bed, especially after their conversation in the afternoon. There'd be no attempt to dissuade him; it was more than Jonty had the heart to attempt.

But Orlando was desperate, taking his lover into his arms the moment they were through the door then hugging him as if he couldn't bear to let him go. The memory of the killings at St. Bride's, never far below the surface, had come back to haunt them both.

"Come on, we'll get ready for bed then I'll sit with you awhile." Jonty kissed his lover's brow, tasting both sweat and fear there.

"Stay with me till morning, please. I'll set the alarm." Orlando cradled his lover's head against his shoulder. "Murder seems to follow us like a hound, Jonty."

"We don't know it is murder. Mr. Ainslie is awaiting the doctor's report—with any luck it will say that it was natural causes." Jonty snuggled into the folds of Orlando's jacket. "Let's play at being Mr. and Mrs. Tattersall, putting on our pyjamas just to lie in bed planning what we'll do tomorrow"

"Croquet." They lay in bed like an old married couple, all thoughts of coupling in any form dissipated. "There's an excellent lawn here. Should I ask them to reserve the set for us?"

Orlando enjoyed that particular game, it being the only sport at which he could beat Jonty with anything like regularity.

"I rather fancied taking a walk to the west of here and finding if there are any little bays where we could bathe on another day." Jonty stopped, seeing a familiar look on his friend's face. "Orlando, why do you always seem so horrified when I suggest bathing? Can you actually swim?"

"I am a very accomplished swimmer, actually, although I'm not keen on the idea of exposing my body to either the elements or public view."

"Not even for me? Not even if I said it would give me the most immense satisfaction to see you in that striped costume, cutting a dash along the strand, dripping wet and gorgeous? Such a mental image to fill one's dreams with."

Orlando applied his knuckles to his lover's head, producing a sharp cry of pain and receiving a punch in the chest in return.

"Amnesty, Orlando! No bathing tomorrow, I promise, just a little healthy exploration of the coast in the morning, then you can thrash me at croquet in the afternoon." Jonty planted a tender kiss on his lover's head, snuggling down next to him to sleep. Murder had driven all the lustful thoughts from his head.

📖

Matthew was wearing a black tie at breakfast. He'd found it in an envelope pushed under his door with a note from Mrs.

Tattersall saying her husband always travelled with one *just in case* and at any rate at their age it *saw a lot of use*. He'd been extremely touched by their kindness, seeking them out as soon as he'd put it on.

"I only wish we could have been of service to you in better circumstances, young man." Mrs. Tattersall's wrinkled face broke into a wistful smile. "If there's anything else we can do, I hope you won't hesitate to tell us."

Matthew promised, grateful if slightly disconcerted at the attention he was receiving. Some kind folk like Dr. Stewart, the Tattersalls and the hotel manager had offered help directly to him; that was fine so long as the proposal wasn't thrust down one's throat. Worse were the sympathetic looks, often accompanied by whispered asides to partners, which smacked of supposition or gossip mongering. Matthew had always sought to keep his affairs to himself, and the possibility of his father's death becoming a public scandal unsettled him.

He watched Jonty and Orlando taking a more leisurely meal, sharing little more than a nod or smile with him. He cursed himself again for his impetuous action. Orlando was damned attractive, but he probably had no interest in anything other than calculus. Matthew ate his breakfast as quickly as was decent, then quietly slipped back to his room to deal with a whole series of business letters that would need drafting.

📖

The morning passed more pleasantly than Orlando had anticipated. Scrambling over rocks to find paths up or down cliffs proved both physically and mentally exhilarating. The views out to sea were stunning. Often he sat with Jonty simply to admire the endless vista of blue, a panorama dotted here and there with fishing boats. Jonty loved the seaside, even more perhaps than he loved London—his obvious delight in the sea air filled Orlando with equal pleasure. They even found a delightful little bay to splash about in whenever someone felt brave enough.

On one occasion when their eyes met, Orlando saw such absolute adoration in his companion's countenance that his heart fair leapt out of his mouth. Intoxicated, he drew Jonty's hand to his face, gently brushing it with his lips, not uttering a word. *Good wine needs no bush and utter happiness no conversation.*

"That's rather bold, isn't it, Orlando? I know no one can see us, but still..."

"Perhaps it is bold, for me. Last night I was reminded of those murders back at Bride's, at what fragile things life and happiness are. This is such a delightful place, it would be wrong not to make the most of it. Together. I'm so used to the security of the college, it's hard for me to adjust to the world at large. Please be patient with me." He choked back the tears which threatened to spoil the occasion.

"Of course I will. Idiot. Let's sit here a while just holding hands, then we'll go back for lunch."

By one o'clock they were on the hotel terrace taking a salad of seafood and local vegetables, which were arranged artfully on their plates in order to tempt the appetite to just the right degree. When a lost-looking Matthew Ainslie appeared, Jonty beckoned him over, earning himself a kick in his shins from Orlando.

"Will you take a bite with us, Mr. Ainslie?" Jonty motioned to the spare seat at their table.

"I will, thank you. Although I insist that you call me Matthew. We're on holiday here, not in a London salon." He attempted a smile but the effort seemed, naturally, half-hearted.

"Then you must call me Jonty. It's an awful name, I know.

Shame one can't have the luxury of naming one's parents in revenge."

Matthew nodded in reply, then turned to his companion, appearing only slightly perturbed at the memory of the previous afternoon. Orlando wondered how he had the gall to address him at all. "I hope you'll call me Matthew, too."

Orlando gritted his teeth. "My name is Orlando, should you wish to use it." He returned to consuming his shellfish, which suddenly didn't taste so pleasant.

Jonty must have seen that it would be entirely up to him to carry the conversation so he turned on the charm while they ate, treading a deft line between mentioning Ainslie senior too much or too little. They chatted as pleasantly as they could manage given the dual presence of grief and a silent Orlando, until Jonty asked whether Matthew had ever visited the racecourse on one of his previous visits to the island, as there was a meeting imminent.

"We were looking forward to going on Friday. My father was a great one for the horses." Matthew suddenly looked older, greyer. "And the tables and the cards."

"Would you still like to? My colleague here is an expert on matters of the gallops so perhaps we could all go together. If you would feel that was the done thing, of course." As Jonty smiled sympathetically, Orlando felt enormously proud of the assured way he was dealing with Matthew's bereavement. There was no excuse for his own surliness—whatever the man had done the day before, he now had a right to be treated with decency.

"I think I'll decline." Matthew shook his head. "Doesn't really seem appropriate. Thank you, anyway."

"Would you like to go to the races again, Orlando? Quite the thing you were last time."

Orlando decided he had to make some effort with the conversation. "Perhaps, Jonty. I do like going racing." Despite himself, he smiled at the memory of being guests of the Stewarts for the Derby, a blustery afternoon spent up on Epsom Downs with Jonty's numerous relatives. Mrs. Stewart had taken him under her wing, refusing to let any of the harridan-like females of the party molest him in any way. He'd been very grateful. When Mr. Stewart had chided her, she'd chastened him with *Dr. Coppersmith doesn't want to run with the fast set as some of your acquaintances do, Richard. You can find the royal party if you wish to indulge in foolery.*

Jonty must have been thinking of the same occasion. "Do you ever go to the Derby, Matthew?"

"My father preferred Ascot. He didn't like the bustle of the Downs. Too common, he thought it."

"I'm afraid my family always wants to picnic up there with the crowds. Mama insists we don't keep aloof—she believes mixing with the gypsies and the hoi polloi is half the fun. Then there's the small matter of keeping us all plied with food from morning till night. Poor Orlando couldn't have eaten another thing."

"I may have been full, but I wasn't daft, was I?" Orlando had almost forgotten the presence of their guest, so rapt was he in the memory of one of the great days of his life.

"There's a story here." Matthew smiled wanly. "Would you care to share it with me? I could do with some light relief."

"Matthew, he had us all fooled. There was me thinking, *Orlando's never been to the races before, so I must make sure he has his wallet safely stowed away and guide him to the bookmakers.*"

Orlando could feel himself blushing, not at the trick he'd pulled on his friend, although he hoped Ainslie would assume it was that. Really it was the memory of the oysters he'd had for lunch that day and how they'd affected him, especially when Jonty had asked, "What do you fancy, then?"

"I asked him on which horse his hard-earned pennies would be going. I was even daft enough to tease him that he'd been using his mathematical skills to the best advantage in spotting the likely winner. Studying form and all that. Do you know what? He had. He'd kept it all secret." Jonty smiled, looking so dashingly handsome that Orlando had the horrible feeling the lobster he'd just consumed was having the same effect as those wretched oysters had done.

"You see, Matthew—" Orlando felt that if he kept his eyes away from Jonty's lovely face he might be able to get things under control, "—one of the St. Bride's porters is a man with a keen appreciation of horseflesh. Mr. Summerbee instructed me in the delights of reading form, studying the weights, picking out the best jockeys and trainers. He even gave me some insider knowledge straight from the gallops at Newmarket, where his brother-in-law is a stable lad."

"Don't forget the fact that those devious porters were supplying you with the Racing Post."

"They are men of great discernment. They wanted me to score off the bookies at the same time as scoring off you. I felt very well prepared, Matthew." Orlando felt the name sticking in his throat, though at least concentrating on that discomfort kept his mind above his waistline. "So I was pretending to choose the horse in the first race just on its name and the jockey's colours. Dr. Stewart took me to his favourite bookmaker so I laid ten shillings 'on the nose' as Summerbee had told me to."

Jonty laughed, attracting the attention of some of the other diners who no doubt felt such levity was inappropriate in the presence of the bereaved. "Chas Satchell and Sons are a firm who've gratefully received my philanthropy in the past. I lose so much they love to keep my custom. I couldn't believe my ears when Orlando used the expression 'on the nose'. I was so stunned I couldn't remember which horse the footman had recommended to me for the first race. I ended up plumping for a rank outsider."

"Did the horse win? Orlando's horse?"

"Of course it did. The family said it was a great case of beginner's luck, even when he looked so unbelievably smug. The bookie didn't mind, of course, having made ample amounts of profit from the rest of us."

"Did the winning streak continue?"

"Oh yes, he steamed up to poor Mr. Satchell muttering things about a horse called Blue Boy and the going being to his liking. I should have twigged then, if not when he went on to pick the winner for the third. We had to go placing our bets all over the shop. I mean to say, my family would have to face Mr. Satchell again at Newmarket. The embarrassment would be too great if he ended up being fleeced." Jonty laughed again, his voice ringing out over the terrace and raising a fond shake of the head from Mrs. Tattersall. "Naturally the whole family wanted his opinion on the Derby."

"I'd come to the conclusion that Spearmint was the one to back..." Orlando began to tell the story, caught a keen look in Matthew's eye then stopped, suddenly feeling uncomfortable. He'd only meant to be polite, to take Jonty's lead in showing companionship to someone who must have been feeling lonely. Now he was blethering on in a manner totally unlike his usual reserved one. Matthew might take his friendliness for interest, then begin once more the nonsense he'd tried the day before. He clammed up tight and, after an awkward pause, Jonty had to resume the story.

"He kept urging caution on everyone about his tip for the big race, saying he was no expert. Everyone laughed at that, of course, suspecting that he was indeed a great connoisseur of horseflesh who was trying to hide his light under a nosebag, if not a bushel. Great quantities of Stewart cash went on that horse, spread over a number of bookies." Jonty looked over at Orlando, who carefully kept his eyes fixed on his plate.

"I shall make sure I take very seriously any advice on horses which you give me, Dr. Coppersmith."

Orlando felt heartened that Matthew had suddenly stopped calling him by his Christian name. He looked up, saying something about his having given up the lure of the bookmakers, otherwise he'd be happy to oblige. It was a relief to see their fellow guest smile then rise from the table.

"Thank you for the story, gentlemen. It was the sort of tonic I needed today."

"I would say it was our pleasure, but that seems unsuitable." Jonty shook the man's hand. "If we can help at all, please let us know."

Orlando continued his triumphs that afternoon on the Beaulieu's croquet lawn. Time after time he sent his friend's blue ball flying into the shrubbery as he made his way remorselessly through the hoops. Jonty didn't mind; it was pleasure enough to see his friend with a determined glint in his eye and a keen look of achievement. While he put every effort into the match, the winning of it was not important. Some would call that Corinthian spirit. He called it love.

He was concentrating hard to produce a delicate shot which would edge his blue ball into proximity to the red one when he felt a hand on his shoulder, followed by a familiar voice in his ear.

"Dr. Stewart, Dr. Coppersmith, what an unexpected pleasure this is."

Both men swung around to see the figure of Inspector

Wilson standing behind them, the man clad in a sporting jacket of as much eminence as their own two. As far as Jonty was concerned, he must have crept up with enormous stealth to achieve just this effect of surprise. He recovered his composure smartly. "The pleasure is all ours, Inspector. Are you taking your holiday here?"

"I am indeed. My sister married a local man. They live not far from here—Mrs. Wilson and I are staying with them. Indeed, Mr. le Tissier is here today in his official capacity, acting for the *connétable*."

"I don't follow you." Jonty found the administrative arrangements of the island as esoteric as those of Cambridge University.

"The head of the parish." Wilson's beaming smile disappeared.

"Oh, Mr. Wilson, please don't tell us that you're here on business?" Jonty's face dropped, while Orlando began to study his croquet mallet.

"Not officially, merely as an adviser to my brother-in-law, who works for the Viscount's Office and so represents the crown. Have you met a Mr. Ainslie here?" The men nodded in reply. "His father died yesterday." More nods of recognition. "I'm afraid he was deliberately killed, a small stiletto-like object inserted into the base of the brain and..." The policeman must have decided discretion was by far the better point of valour so skipped the anatomical details. "It seems we begin again gentlemen, on the trail of a murderer. I expect that you will be taking a keen interest in matters?" Wilson's eyes glinted.

Orlando looked up. "You wish for the pair of us to keep our eyes and ears open?" He had an inquisitive spark in his eye that spoke volumes.

"I *was* going to advise you to keep well clear of the case, however I thought better of it. Too combative by half, you two, I remembered that as soon as I saw you whacking that ball into the shrubbery. Now, before I start in there—" the inspector tipped his head towards the hotel, "—one or two questions..."

Chapter Four

Matthew was halfway down the stairs when he heard two men introducing themselves to Greenwood. One was a mainland policeman, the other was clearly some local officer; he didn't need to eavesdrop on why they were here. Arrangements were being made to interview all present at the Beaulieu, so the natural thing would have been to return to his room to await their call. Matthew didn't want that pleasure just yet, so he slipped into the lounge, finding a nook where he could attempt to gather his thoughts.

The rotten luck that seemed to be dogging him was obviously still on his trail. Rather than going off sleuthing, the two policemen entered the room and stood by the window. Matthew prayed he would remain unobserved.

"Your old pals, eh?" Le Tissier watched the two croquet players. "A more suspicious man might take a wary view of their appearance at another murder scene."

"I am a more suspicious man, George. There are small bells jingling in my brain. I was chary of them during our investigations at St. Bride's." Wilson narrowed his eyes as if trying to see through the glass, over the terrace and into the Cambridge fellows' brains.

"But you invited them in to help you."

"We did. It was partly curiosity, partly instinct, partly because I wished to keep a close eye on them. However, they had a faultless alibi for the second crime—thirty members of St. Thomas's Senior Common Room can't all have been lying. Now here they are again, lurking about another murder scene. I'd advise you look at their explanation very carefully."

"I will. You know, I don't hold much store with alibis. I once came across a murderer who produced forty people who said he was in the dining room of an eminent hotel at the time of the crime. It was the testimony of the forty-first man, who'd seen him enter the house in question, which brought about a confession."

"Their being here might be nothing more than coincidence. There's many twists of fate which would look farfetched if set down in fiction." Wilson's shrewd gaze implied he didn't hold much store by coincidence.

"We'd better get down to it, then, the slog of establishing everyone's whereabouts on Monday afternoon. At least it'll give us a clearer view of what's going on in the hotel community."

As if on cue, Greenwood arrived to usher the policemen into a private room, giving Matthew the chance to escape from his hiding place. So the men from Cambridge did a bit of amateur sleuthing, did they? That was something which needed careful consideration, especially when Jonty had been so free with his offers of help. Matthew was going to have to find out a bit more on that front—he had a good idea who to ask—before he let himself get any closer to this intriguing pair.

He was still lost in thought when Wilson called him to answer some questions. Matthew's explanation of all that had gone on the day before proved, judging by the policemen's faces, unsatisfactory.

Le Tissier questioned with great determination, focussing on the period after Matthew had told them he'd last seen his father. "You took lunch, then he retired to your suite and you went to play tennis. You'd booked one of the tennis courts yet you say that you didn't end up playing. Why?"

"As I've already told you, Dr. Coppersmith and I had a difference of opinion before the match could start. I returned to our suite to find my father dead. I assume that Dr. Coppersmith returned to his room."

"According to the man himself—" Wilson consulted his notepad, "—you didn't play because you made a suggestion he found objectionable."

"What suggestion?" The prickles of anxiety on Matthew's neck grew more intense.

"He wouldn't say. His exact words were *I'm sure it has no relevance in this case, although it was something ungentlemanly. He'd said he wanted to show me the honey buzzards. Honey buzzards, my aunt Fanny.* We reminded him that we would decide what was relevant."

"Could this difference of opinion have concerned cheating at cards?" Le Tissier had a cold, keen eye. Matthew felt as if he were a creature under a microscope.

"I beg your pardon?"

"Someone has told us that on Sunday night they were fairly certain, although without proof, your father was attempting to do something at the bridge table, perhaps trying to see other players' hands."

This was too close to home. "I can't say what my father was attempting that night. My mind was on my cards. I will admit that he had been known in the past as a sharp player." Matthew wondered who could have made the allegations. His thoughts came immediately to Orlando; Jonty would be far too gentlemanly. The prickles of tension were turning to nausea.

"We've also been told there was an atmosphere between your father and you. Can you tell us what it was about?"

Matthew rose onto unsteady feet. "I can, but not now. You will excuse me, I feel quite unwell..."

Dinner was a quiet affair for everyone, conversation subdued, beds sought early. The only really happy note for Orlando was the downturn of the barometer and therefore the distinct possibility that bathing couldn't happen on Wednesday. The two eminent fellows of St. Bride's lay in bed listening to a gentle summer shower caress the window panes. There was no question now of sleeping apart again this fortnight, irrespective of what else happened in the bed. Their affection had gone far beyond sole reliance on physical delights—the intimacy of body and soul had become indivisible. Orlando reclined on his front, elbows on the bed, chin in hands, reading a book on calculus which Jonty had hidden fifteen times but which had still mysteriously made its way into their luggage.

Jonty was supposed to be communing with *The Moonstone*, an old favourite which he regarded as an immense comfort. Instead he was admiring his lover's shoulders. "When I was a young boy I used to be taken to the Museum of Natural History. It was my favourite treat, even more so than the zoo—of course I was too young for the theatre then. I adored the glyptodont carapace. I had visions of being a renowned palaeontologist, going off to find equally amazing fossils to delight children with. I would caress his back—it wasn't as smooth as yours, Orlando—then tell him all sorts of secrets. Now please don't laugh because I've never told anyone this before."

Orlando had begun to giggle at the mention of the words "glyptodont carapace", not exactly the sort of expression he expected to hear from the mouth of his lover. "Who do you tell your secrets to now? You don't seem that keen on the *Iguanodon* down with the other geological specimens at the museum, so *he* can't be privy to your innermost thoughts."

"Don't have any secrets any more. I've got you and I tell you everything." He caressed Orlando's back, as if the man were as prime a specimen as any nine-year-old budding zoologist could desire. "Don't want to try to seduce you tonight; want to rub your back while you read your book and daydream a bit. No beds like this back at the college, so I want to make the most of every moment."

Orlando smiled affectionately, then assumed his more usual concerned look. "Shame about this murder business, though. Hasn't got you too worried?"

"Strangely enough, given the events of last February, the answer is *no*. Exhilarated, I would say, rather than frightened. The thrill of the chase and all that." Jonty's eyes lit up. "As close as we came to death last time, the thought of applying our brains to another mystery stimulates me."

"Would you be happy if we got involved?" Orlando was still concerned. They'd had a brush with death last time, in the form of a razor-wielding maniac

"Are you saying that you wouldn't want to get mixed up in this, because I don't believe it for one moment. You'd want to poke your rather attractive nose in, too."

Orlando blushed, having been fathomed out again. "You know me too well." He looked up, held Jonty's gaze. "I don't want a repeat of what happened last time, though. You're not to put yourself into danger."

"I promise. I won't let anyone in the room, bar you or the chambermaid—so I hope she isn't the culprit. I'll avoid all people with sharp objects, even Mrs. Tattersall with her knitting needles or the manager with that ghastly tiepin." He laughed, returning to doodling with his finger on Orlando's back, while the man in question returned to his beloved numbers.

Jonty didn't dare suggest that they share the bed in a more romantically constructive way. He was too afraid of being snubbed again.

The day did dawn grey, with something akin to a nip in the air. Orlando tried very hard not to appear smug and even offered to visit any place his friend chose to name in recompense. Even churches. At this, Jonty's eyes regained a bit of their gleam, sadly lost when he'd seen the gloomy skies. He plumped for a day of visiting the Town Church in St. Helier, then taking the railway up to Grouville for a walk over the common and then up to the harbour. Orlando didn't mind, so long as donning the striped bathing suit was still avoided. He would also have enjoyed a little amateur sleuthing if the chance came up, but didn't want to press the subject.

As with the first set of murders they'd been involved in, the two men didn't have to go seeking for evidence; it wanted to come to them unasked, like a paper clip to a magnet. By the time they reached St. Helier, they knew more about Ainslie senior than they could ever have hoped for.

They met one of their fellow guests—Mr. Sheringham, father of the spinster who rather resembled a horse—at St. Aubin's station. He'd been abandoned by his wife and daughter who were meeting a very hearty female friend, one with no time for males. He expressed his pleasure at having the two younger men to chat with as he travelled. He also rejoiced in having been the only man able to tell the police that he "already knew, well, knew of, Charles Ainslie" and had been "able to tell them a thing or two, or three".

These things Mr. Sheringham shared with his two new friends. "Not that I want to speak ill of the dead," he averred, which indicated that was exactly what he intended to do, "but Ainslie had been blackballed by a London club because he wasn't trusted at cards."

More revelations followed, Ainslie in his youth having been banned from one of the Riviera gambling dens because of alleged irregularities at the tables. He'd been implicated in the separation of Lord and Lady Hardley because of his familiarity with her ladyship.

"Furthermore, they say that twenty years ago he accused a certain gentleman, good North Country stock, of cheating at the card table. The matter would have come to court had the chap in question not been killed in a tragic accident cleaning his gun. He'd made a few enemies, I would guess, our Mr. Ainslie." Sheringham ended his character assassination as the train pulled into the station, allowing him to take his leave on the platform.

Jonty snorted. "I'd love to know how much of that tirade Wilson and his brother-in-law actually believed. Because I know for a fact that Lord Hardley ran away to set up home with the parlour maid—had that titbit from my mother so there can be no arguing with it. If Sheringham's wrong on that count he could be wrong on them all. Except the bit about making enemies, that would be very likely."

"An act of vengeance then?" Orlando shivered slightly in remembrance of the vengeful murders in St. Bride's earlier in the year.

"Quite likely. Terrible thing, the need to exact your own kind of justice. That's why I would never tell either you or my father the names of those boys who hurt me at school. Between the pair of you, you'd destroy them." He managed a small smile. "Still, the game's afoot, eh, Dr. Coppersmith? Wonder if we can find anyone else at the hotel who knew Charles Ainslie, yet hasn't admitted the fact to the police?"

"That would probably be a better hare to course than chasing alibis."

"True. I bet most people couldn't produce corroborative evidence of their location on Monday. That young married couple probably couldn't speak about what *they'd* been doing."

"Language, Jonty, we're in public. You still think it wasn't his son?" Orlando frowned at the thought of Matthew Ainslie. He still wouldn't trust him with a loaf of bread let alone another man's life. And he'd been the last to see his father alive—it didn't mean he'd left him alive.

"I doubt he did it. I saw how he looked that Monday night. Bleak would be the word, or shattered. The man would have to be a wonderful actor to reproduce the expressions and colours I've seen on his face the last two days. There was tension between the pair of them, yes, but I don't think Matthew killed his father. It'll be like it was before. The last person we suspect will be the killer."

It was Orlando's turn to grimace. "It'll probably turn out to be the manager, who objected to the way the man complained about the salmon on Sunday." It was a reasonable reply, so he hoped Jonty hadn't heard the sudden tension in his voice, the distress that must be showing on his face when the relationship between Ainslie's father and son had been mentioned. He'd neatly changed the subject, hoping that the possibility of being asked *what was your father like?* had been avoided again.

It hadn't. "What was your father like, Orlando?"

He bridled. "Why must we spoil this day with memories of the past? I thought you wanted to see the church." He strode on ahead, leaving his friend to come along in his wake like a sturdy frigate to a ship of the line.

They reached the church without further talk and Jonty tried to bring Orlando out of his shell by getting him to translate the Latin inscriptions. By the time they'd looked at every brass or tablet in the place, Orlando felt almost civil again. They took a moment to sit in the pews, enjoying the watery light which filtered through the stained glass.

Bloodhound Stewart was obviously still on the trail, not easily shaken off. "I know that it'll hurt to talk of this, but it'll hurt us even more if we don't. I have very few secrets from you,

you know the depths of my despair and the summits of my joys. I don't know a thing about your childhood so I'm beginning to imagine all sorts of terrible things that must be much worse than the reality. Share it with me, please, as much as you can bear to tell me now." His eyes looked just as pleading as they had back in the Fellows' Garden when he'd wanted to take the first steps towards healing.

Orlando's heart was melted; in the thaw, the story poured out. It was a tale of a repressive childhood which seemed to consist entirely of *Thou shalt not.* A boy who hadn't been allowed to make his own friends and who'd rejected his parents' choice of acquaintances for him. A boy immersed in studies or sport, both seen as being a potential means to escape, to release the tension. A mother who couldn't or wouldn't—or wasn't allowed to—tell her only son that she loved him, either in words or with a kiss. A father who ruled his family with the rod.

Orlando felt the hot, angry tears welling in his eyes and was thankful when his friend proffered a handkerchief just in case. He shook his head, took a huge breath, tried to smile. "It's such a relief to tell you all this, Jonty, not to be always having to try to change the subject or stall. I feel such a burden has been taken off my back."

"I think we can risk this." Jonty squeezed his friend's hand. "Only God and his angels to see us. I'm fairly sure they won't mind." They sat for a while not talking, then set off for the Snow Hill station in order to take the train north into unknown territory.

Orlando had been constantly amazed this holiday that such a small island could contain such a variety of landscapes—this trip was no disappointment. They walked over the windy common, then followed the edge of the beach up to the harbour, stomachs rumbling all the while.

Jonty seemed to have some definite end in mind, steering them towards an old tavern by the quay, where they were entertained to lunch by an old porter from St. Bride's who had taken over the inn from his father. While Orlando enjoyed the beer greatly, the mackerel pâté even more, the stories of Jonty's undergraduate days were best of all.

From the moment the landlord greeted him with, "I can't recall the name, but aren't you the lad who brought the goat into the porters' lodge?" Orlando knew the trip had been worthwhile. It was even better to discover that this misdemeanour had cost Jonty a gating plus two crates of ale. By the time they reached the tale about the three umbrellas and the bicycle, Orlando was beaming, contemplating slipping their host a guinea in return for a written account of all the things that Jonty had been in trouble for in his youth. He was thwarted by Jonty insisting they take an immediate, rather tipsy, leave. The two men wandered home happily, picking wildflowers en route with which to decorate their suite.

Dinner was slightly livelier that evening. Matthew was dining at the Tattersalls' table, having spent the day answering correspondence and phone calls from the mainland, when he wasn't answering questions from the police.

They'd called him again, forcing him into admitting that he'd attempted to embrace Orlando, an embrace he insisted was just friendly but had been misunderstood. He said he'd been feeling unwell, been under nervous strain from work and had acted out of character. The admission had inevitably led to a long discussion about whether this strain had caused an equal tension with his father. Did Charles Ainslie know about his son's altercation with the other male guest? Had Matthew been feeling unwell because he'd just dug a stiletto into his father's brain stem?

Jonty kept an eye on the trio. Matthew looked tired and

being fussed over by Mrs. T didn't seem to be making him any happier—likely he'd had enough of feminine bustling as he'd been the subject of much sympathy by the "Misses" Sheringham and Forbes in the bar before dinner. Jonty felt enormous compassion for the man, despite his having attempted to seduce Orlando. He wondered what could have driven Matthew to be so reckless as to kiss another man in broad daylight, albeit in the cover of the trees. A desire to shock his father in some way? Desperation of some sort, or fervent emotion? He hoped it wasn't passion unleashed after some blazing row which had ended up in the death of his father.

At least Jonty could hazard a pretty good guess at what had egged Matthew on. He could just imagine Orlando during the conversation about Oscar Wilde in the bar—being clueless, missing the subtle signs of someone manifesting their attraction to him, nodding in exactly the wrong places and making the insinuation that he would be interested in an encounter. Orlando still had an awful lot to learn about life.

Jonty looked at his lover with great tenderness. He'd done well today, relating the terribly lonely, harshly repressed times of his childhood. Jonty still wanted to ask the burning questions *Why did your father cut his throat? Why do it in front of you?* He knew the incident had sent his lover into a self-constructed shell for the next thirteen years and had shortened his mother's life considerably. He wanted to know more, but Orlando had come so far this day, his spirit still intact, that Jonty wouldn't risk upsetting this particular applecart by asking now. He'd learn the answers some day.

"Penny for your thoughts?" Orlando was licking the last piece of crème caramel from his spoon, in preparation for attacking a scalding hot coffee.

"Just thinking about chains of events, the little subtle chances or decisions that might go one way or another and that end up changing the entire world. Like if I'd taken up the offer to go to University College, Dublin rather than St. Bride's."

Orlando stared down at his empty plate, Jonty registering the familiar signs of distress. He knew it always upset him to think about the fact they might never have met.

Luckily the coffee arrived and with it a note in the instantly recognisable handwriting of Inspector Wilson. Orlando passed the note to Jonty, raising an inquisitive eyebrow. Among the chitchat was the smallest casual hint that the fellows might keep their eyes and ears open, especially in the direction of Ainslie junior. If they also came across anything regarding the hotel manager (who was known to have worked in the club where Ainslie senior had been blackballed) or Mr. Forbes, who was involved with a rival publishing business, then that would be very handy, too.

Jonty whistled. "Seems he does want the stable gossip again, just as he hinted yesterday. At least we can legitimately snoop around now—I know you're desperate to." The little smirk in reply told him he was absolutely right.

Coffee was drunk, then port, and so at last came bed. As the two men reached the foot of the staircase, Jonty glanced at the barometer. "Set fair for tomorrow, Orlando. Those bathing outfits will be getting an airing, I'll warrant."

Orlando sighed, staring defeat in the face. "I dare say they will, but the logistics of the exercise worry me."

"You needn't be concerned, it'll all be under control."

Orlando wouldn't be so easily put off and the conversation continued in bed. "How precisely are we to get ourselves into these costumes, Jonty? There aren't any bathing machines in that little cove."

"I think that we should be rather daring, and have them on under our normal clothes. Then we can go into that little clump of trees at the back and disrobe. No one is likely to be there to see us—if they were, we'd have to be eminently discreet. We're used to being that, aren't we?"

Orlando grimaced. "The mere thought of unbuttoning my flies in public, irrespective of whether I'm behind a bush and wearing a full bathing costume underneath, is horrifying. How does your plan work for getting us back into our everyday clothes afterwards?"

"Ah, there's the rub. Might have to utilise those bushes again or some big towels. We take turns on watch and hope the wind doesn't gust if a lady walks past." Jonty was pleased to see his lover's jaw drop as far as his chest. He was getting fewer opportunities these days to shock him; now he relished every one. "It really is quite simple to keep covered if you're quick about it. Anyway, who would want to look at your great long strip of a body? You're just like a streak of water out of the tap. More meat on a butcher's pencil."

Orlando grabbed Jonty and pulled him down onto the soft mattress. "Just because certain people around here are built like a carthorse, they shouldn't make insinuations about other people's physiques. There may be very little meat on me, Dr. Stewart, but what there is, is prime fillet. Would you be interested in a practical demonstration?"

Jonty sighed languorously. At last, at long last, Orlando had relaxed enough to want to make love again, away from his safe haven. They hadn't done so since a few days before they'd left St. Bride's—it seemed a much longer time of abstinence. "I thought you would never ask. Yes, please."

"Well it's tough for you because you're not getting one." Orlando rose from the bed, taking his half-naked and offended body back to its own room.

Jonty didn't know whether to laugh or cry. This was what he'd always wanted of his lover, someone who could give as good as he got, who would stand up to him with a bit of sparring. It was a shame he'd chosen to fight back over such an intimate matter.

Jonty waited five minutes—that was usually enough time for an ordinary storm to blow over—then made his way to his friend's room. This was the second time within a few days that he'd been forced to knock apologetically on this particular door. His welcome was no warmer than it had been previously.

"Body not available, Dr. Stewart," came the answer from inside the room. "It's taken umbrage at the insult and wants to be left alone."

"Not after your body," Jonty lied. "I wanted to offer to read to you from that nice book about differential calculus. I won't do any silly voices this time or overemphasise words that might have a double meaning." He poked his head tentatively round the doorframe. This might just work, as Orlando loved the sound of his voice and to listen to him intoning mathematical vocabulary was as pleasant for the man as to hear him reciting a sonnet. But he seemed suspicious now.

"I know what you're up to. You want to get onto my bed then read to me until I'm lulled into a congenial mood. You know that I'll fall for you hook, line and sinker all over again. Even here. Even away from St. Bride's. You're dangerous."

Jonty couldn't help grinning guiltily. "You know me too well. I promise that this time I'll only read and I'll go back to my own room at any point you ask me to." He picked up the little mathematical volume, flicking idly through it to a well-thumbed page. "I also promise that tomorrow I'll guard your body as if it were the crown jewels themselves. Not a single eye will see any unseemly part of it, although I have to say I think you have no unseemly parts at all. Every one of them is beautiful and if there is the slightest chance that you change your mind about a practical demonstration of my admiration, I'll be more than happy to oblige." He couldn't prevent himself from launching into a huge smirk.

"I've warned you once already that I will not be gulled into having sex with you tonight."

Jonty's eyebrows leapt up into his hairline. He'd never heard his friend refer to lovemaking in such blunt terms before. "Orlando! What sort of a book can that *Bleak House* be to cause you to use such language?"

"There's no one in Dickens who could drive me to such terms, just a lavender-pyjama-clad imp who insists on coming into my room to seduce me at every possible opportunity." Despite his earlier words, he motioned Jonty to join him on the bed then gently took his hand. "You produce such emotions in me as I never thought possible. There are occasions when all I can think of is how quickly I can get into a convenient bed with you. I worry that everyone will look at me and know that's what I'm thinking."

Jonty shook his head, gently stroking the hand which held his. "They never will, Orlando. You hide your emotions so well, even from me."

"There are times when I feel the need to expose my soul entirely to you. I have such thoughts come into my head, such words on my lips. When we're at our most intimate, I want so badly to say things which are disgraceful." Orlando's eyes were fixed on his hands, probably, Jonty thought, in case they should go off doing something naughty if he didn't keep then constantly under view.

"You can say anything to me—use any words, voice any thought. I'll neither judge you nor condemn." Jonty drew his hand down Orlando's cheek, his neck, his chest. The silk of his pyjamas felt cool, as soft as the skin beneath. "That's what love is about. Absolute trust."

A brief look of fear flicked across Orlando's face. "Trust has its dangers, Jonty. Ainslie must have trusted the man who killed him. If he knew he was meeting an implacable enemy he wouldn't have let him go around the back of him with a blade in his hand, would he? That's what was so effective with the St. Bride's murderer." He stopped short when he remembered what

Jonty's trust had led to in that case.

"You're right, of course. We should have spotted him. I know we've gone through it before but all the evidence was under our noses. Somehow we ignored it."

Orlando mirrored the movement of his lover's hand, caressing Jonty's face, neck, chest with his long, nimble, capable fingers. "We won't make that mistake this time."

"Indeed we won't. Come, I promised to read that book to you and I count that as binding. My reward will be anything you choose to give me."

"You can have your reward now." Orlando leaned forward, kissing Jonty affectionately, then with increasing passion. This wasn't a goodnight-see-you-in-the-morning kiss. This was a the-night-is-young-and-so-are-we type of kiss. He fiddled with Jonty's jacket buttons. "I'm sorry I've not wanted to...to make love to you. Have I been a big idiot again?"

"No. Not really." Jonty lightly caressed Orlando's hand. "It's like the old thing about hiding a letter in a letter rack. Where's the best place to hide a pair of men who want to be together all the time? In a Cambridge college. Away from St. Bride's it's different. Here caution isn't foolishness." He moved his hand to stroke his lover's knee. "You must admit, though, we've established by now that no one's likely to come barging through our locked door, so it wouldn't be foolhardy to risk lovemaking." He turned Orlando's face towards him. "I really would value it."

"Then we'll make it so." Orlando started undoing the buttons he'd been fiddling with.

Jonty could feel the prickles of excitement on his neck, like a sprinkle of raindrops. It had been a long, dry spell, a time of constantly searching the sky of his lover's demeanour for a cloud of desire. A cloud which might be persuaded to burst into a sweet rain of passion. Jonty felt parched, arid, desperate to be drenched in the downpour. "The light, Orlando. Let's put it out."

In the warm, hushed darkness, Orlando's hands once more found his lover's body. He lowered his head, planting kisses on Jonty's chest, working up, over the shoulders, onto his back. Jonty revelled in the cascade of kisses, turning his head to better take pleasure in the sweet, moist touch of his lover's lips. He caressed the soft skin of Orlando's back, tracing the same lazy circles as he often did, the motions which they both relished so much and which made them so thrilled.

"Orlando, you've been so brave this holiday. Leaving the college, sharing a double bed, so many new things." Jonty's voice was hoarse. "Would you be brave enough to try something else new, for me?"

Orlando froze, the sudden tension in his muscles speaking as loudly as any whispered "No, I'm still frightened" might have done. "I...I'm not sure. Not yet." He forced the words out.

"Then let me kiss you." Jonty, disappointed but at least still hopeful of something if not the ultimate consummation, whispered into the charged, electrical air that flowed between them, air like the strange atmosphere that preceded thunder. Only this ambience promised a storm without lightning.

"No, this is your reward. You can kiss me later, bring me pleasure later, now it's all for you. My love," Orlando murmured into his lover's neck, gracing it again with kisses, "my only love."

Jonty lay back, letting himself be soaked in delight, allowing his lover's fingers and mouth to run free, trying to dispel any guilt at the selfish hedonism he felt. His lover had offered freely, he wanted it to be so. Jonty knew that despite all Orlando had said these last few days, his unconscious body longed for them to make love again. As they'd slept side by side, he'd been aware of his lover's excitement, of his being, as Orlando put it—poor shy Orlando who had to rely on coy euphemisms—"ready to do his duty". They were both *ready to do their duty* now, imminently so on Jonty's part, especially if

Orlando kept touching there, now.

"Please stop a moment." Jonty moved his lover's hand away. "No, it's all right, I just wanted the chance to relax a while. Get my breath back." He brushed his hand along his lover's pyjamas. "Take these off, eh?"

He lay back again, breathing deeply. It was wrong, after such a drought, to let the first tempest blow out in such a short space of time. They should calm down again, make the storm last until they both yearned for the thunder to crash, bringing peace and satiation.

Jonty felt Orlando's smooth frame sidle up to him again, sleek with sweat. "Together, please? I don't mind playing games, but tonight is special, our first time away from college. It should be concurrent, not sequential, any good mathematician should know that." He heard his lover chuckle in the darkness.

"As you wish. Always as you wish." Orlando began to pay his attentions again, letting Jonty respond in kind this time.

It was better, so much better, to give and take pleasure in concert. Orlando's skin tasted sweet, as did his hair. His silky skin delighted Jonty's fingers as much as Orlando's fingers thrilled his flesh. The trickles of delight became streams, and the streams became torrents of exhilaration.

"Sh, sh," Jonty whispered into his lover's ear. Orlando had begun to moan, just a little too loudly—the walls here weren't as thick as the stone of St. Bride's. "This isn't the place." He brought his fingers up to Orlando's lips, holding them there.

"I'm sorry," Orlando murmured against his friend's hand. "Should we stop?"

"No!" Jonty wasn't sure he could stop, not now. "No, just keep the noise down. If you can," he added, smiling affectionately.

Orlando became quieter. Jonty could feel his lover's mouth pressed against his shoulder as the tempest reached its crescendo. He wondered whether the man was trying to repress the urge to cry out. One day he'd take him to his family home in Sussex, with its thick walls and long corridors, but for now they'd have to be canny.

Jonty whispered more words of affection, broken whispers because it had got close to the point where he'd hardly be able to speak.

"Make it happen, Jonty." Orlando breathed the words into his lover's hair. The plaintive note in his voice made Jonty's heart turn a somersault. Making love to Orlando over the last few months had proved a revelation, the man having depths of emotion that could hardly be guessed at by looking at his stern exterior. If he was serious and shy in the outside world, in bed he was strong yet sensitive, as bold as Thor with thunderbolts of passion, as tender as a fawn. Now he was like a child again, a little boy who'd found an amazing gift—love—and the equally amazing acts of love which could enfold it.

"Of course, Orlando. I do love you, you know." Jonty's hands began to make the final little motions that would make the storm reach its climax, then be done. He almost didn't need Orlando to do the same for him; to bring his lover pleasure was going to be enough, this time.

As the peak came, just as a summer shower suddenly hit the windows and serenaded them with soft pattering, they didn't need to swear their love to each other, protest the fullness of it, as they both already knew that fact well enough.

Chapter Five

"Just go behind the bush and take your trousers off. Now."
Jonty's patience had worn dangerously thin because someone
was prevaricating. The *someone* still refused to move. "If you
don't do it within the next ten seconds, I will come and do it for
you. I mean it. I'll strip you down to your bathing costume in
full view of *everyone*, then I'll take all my clothes off—*all* of
them, Orlando. Then I'll probably shout, just to bring attention
to ourselves."

It was a hollow threat. The everyone was actually three sea
gulls and a sad-looking cormorant. The only people who could
have paid any attention were on two fishing trawlers and they'd
have needed powerful telescopes to see anything in the secluded
little cove.

But empty as it was, the warning had been enough to get
Orlando scurrying behind the shrubs while his friend kept
watch, eventually emerging in a glorious blue-and-white
horizontally striped costume. One which he felt did justice to
his lithe frame.

"About time, too. That water looks so enticing, some of us
could have been in it ten minutes ago." Jonty continued to
mutter as he went behind the bush, flinging his suit and shirt
off.

Jonty filled his costume very effectively, so much so that
Orlando had to look away for a few moments to compose

himself. He had seen this extraordinary sight before, of course, when they'd donned the handsome garments after breakfast, but he'd been too full of worry to take any notice. Now Jonty was looking devastatingly attractive and he couldn't do a thing about it. Except remember how wonderful the last night had been, perhaps anticipate the next.

There had been a nasty moment as they left the hotel, when they'd run into the "Misses", as Jonty now referred to the two young unmarried ladies who were staying at the Beaulieu. The girls had been particularly inquisitive about how the men were to spend their day. Orlando had silently prayed that his normally scrupulously honest friend wouldn't reveal their secret, making it impossible not to invite the females along. He'd underestimated the man's ingenuity; Jonty had told the ladies they were intending to study Scyphozoan life forms, with perhaps a diversionary examination of the native Reptilia, which had been quite enough to put the girls off. It was to Orlando's great good fortune that the bag they carried, though stuffed with towels and clean underwear, resembled a zoological specimen sack.

"We will look for jellyfish," Jonty had said once they were heading along the coast, "and lizards too, but not until we've swum in the sea." His eyes had sparkled at the prospect.

Those same eyes had dulled considerably after Orlando's display of skittishness concerning fly buttons. They were now regaining luminosity. "Race you to the sea!" Pushing him out of the way to get a head start, Jonty bounded off towards the waves. He'd counted without Orlando's exceptional turn of speed—he had overtaken him, dodgy Achilles' tendon notwithstanding, by the time they reached the wet sand. They raced headlong into the water until the waves hit their chests, making Orlando splutter.

"Just a bit cold, eh, Jonty?"

"You'll soon get used to it. This is glorious." Jonty bounced energetically as the waves broke on his body, encouraging his friend to do the same.

Once they were almost immersed in the sea, the shock of the cold lessened, providing a pleasant contrast to the heat of the day. The water was beautifully clean and seaweed-free in this little cove, allowing a clear sight to the shell-strewn sea floor. They soon decided to risk swimming, just a short distance at first, then in great widths across the bay, resting on the rocks in between laps.

"Bracing, Dr. Coppersmith?"

"Marvellous, Dr. Stewart."

All morning was spent in the water until the rumblings of Jonty's internal stomach alarm indicated that lunch was required. The picnic the hotel had provided was rummaged out of the zoologist's sack, to be laid out on the flat stones at the back of the beach. The men had insisted on simple fare— sandwiches, fruit, and bottles of beer—but in this setting, with the glorious weather, they felt like Adam and Eve feasting on the fruits of a yet unsullied paradise.

Perhaps this was what it felt like in Eden before the fall, Orlando reflected, which was an odd thought considering that it was Jonty who was the religious one.

After lunch they lay on their stomachs on the warm, flat rocks, watching the green lizards scuttling along the paths like little liquid emeralds. The sun beat down on their backs, the air smelled sweet and they both had the most precious thing in their lives next to them. It felt exactly like the February day when they'd sat in the Fellows' Garden weeping away the majority of the hurt they'd suffered during the "St. Bride's Murders", as the *News of the World* had referred to them.

The process of recovery had gone on a lot longer, of course. Jonty's family had noticed the change in him when he'd joined them for Easter, Orlando in tow. The smile and the easy banter couldn't entirely mask the reserve they hadn't seen during his previous visit. Not to mention the nervous young man at his side, who felt like he was being taken to the Spanish Inquisition rather than staying with an aristocratic family as their guest. Orlando knew he'd been mentioned in many a letter or the occasional telephone call, but he'd wondered how they would react to the contrast he made with their own fun-loving son. He needn't have worried and now he remembered the time with great fondness.

Much of what had happened during their visit he only found out second hand. How Jonty had quietly taken his parents aside, calmly explaining to them all the winter's events. The murders, the threat to his own life. His mother had cried at the thought of her most beloved boy having a razor held to his throat, although she'd apparently seemed pleased to see the look of tenderness which swept over Jonty's face every time he spoke of his dearest friend. Mr. Stewart, shocked at the events that had rocked St. Bride's, his own college, had patted his son on the shoulder over again, murmuring, "Brave boy, very proud of you."

Orlando suddenly jolted back into consciousness. He'd been thinking about the trip to the Stewart's home, had fallen asleep and dreamed the whole experience again, vividly seeing and hearing Jonty's parents, tasting the food, smelling the fresh flowers which had always been in his bedroom. Happy days. These were happy days too, despite a murder and an unwanted suitor.

He looked fondly down at the blond head that lay beside his. Jonty snored quietly, seeming for all the world as if he were twelve years old and without a care. Mercifully the small copse of trees gave them enough shade to avoid the risk of burning, allowing them to gently bask like the lizards they'd been observing. Orlando thanked the God in whom he didn't believe for being so gracious as to give him such joy.

He watched while Jonty gradually came to, shaking the sleep out of his head and rubbing his eyes like a small boy. This was how he always awoke, and it gave Orlando great joy to observe the little rituals his lover engaged in. He waited for the expected stretch of the arms—it came—the turning on his side—that came too—then the familiar words. "Hello, Orlando. Lovely to see you." Jonty stretched again. "Been dreaming?"

"I was thinking about Easter at your parents' house."

"Happy times." Jonty giggled. "I remember the first two days, your incessant thinking made the house seem filled with brooding. You were so worried."

"I was scared they'd hate me. Or guess about us." Orlando shivered at the thought, even though the day was at its warmest point.

"They loved you. Mama was totally besotted, still is. Papa likes you enormously." He grinned furtively. "And of course they've guessed."

"What?" A bolt of fear shot up Orlando's spine. For all the sunshine, he was suddenly very cold.

"Well, they couldn't have had us as guests twice over and not guessed, could they? They're not daft." Jonty studied his hands. "Actually, I told them. I meant to tell you before, but you always seemed so skittish about it that..."

Orlando felt as if his head would explode. He respected the Stewarts greatly, was beginning to feel the sort of affection for them he'd never had for his own parents. He'd never guessed they *knew*. "When did you tell them? On Derby day?"

"No, back at Easter. By the time you were their guest at Epsom, they knew exactly how things stood. It didn't make a difference to the hospitality you received, did it?"

Orlando had to admit it didn't; he'd been treated just like a son, those marvellous few days. It made no sense to him. "I could never have told my parents anything like that had they still been living, Jonty. The repercussions wouldn't have borne thinking about. They'd have thrown me out of the house, my mother wailing at the disgrace I'd brought upon the family. My father...I suspect my father would have marched me to the police and had me up in court. Probably would have regretted I wasn't in Nelson's navy so I could have been hung from the yardarm." Orlando shivered again, closing his arms around himself.

Jonty responding by cuddling him close. The bushes which gave them shade gave them plenty of privacy. "I've been blessed with a very understanding family for which I regularly thank God. I can only guess how different it must have been for you."

"You haven't the slightest idea." Orlando drew his lover's head towards him, ruffling his hair. "Did you ever tell your parents about Richard Marsters?"

"Of course I did, Orlando. How else would they have taken the news about you without so much as batting an eyelid?" Jonty smiled. "It was when I was in my second year as an undergraduate. When I'd made the decision to tell my parents what had happened at school."

Orlando was astonished again. "You hadn't told them before?"

"No. I'd hoped that keeping silent about it at the time would make it feel like it had never happened. If no one else knew, I could pretend it was all a bad dream. Or a series of them, punctuated by thunder and tears. But I grew up; Richard had helped me to regain my confidence, as had being such a success on the rugby field. Telling all to him had made a huge difference to my feelings about myself, cleansing the guilt, getting rid of the dirt, so I felt that telling my parents would take the healing process further on."

For all that Orlando rarely spoke of his own childhood—he still couldn't open up some of the deepest parts of his life—he'd taken infinite pains to support his lover in sharing his own troubles. "Did it, Jonty? Did opening up help?" The question hadn't just been asked for form's sake. Orlando needed some reassurance that if he ever exposed his own history, completely, it would be a healing and not a harmful act.

"I should have done it years before, truly. It was a terrible shock to them, of course, Mother crying buckets as usual. For a woman who is built like, even acts like, the *Dreadnought*, she can be remarkably soppy. I do love her." He smiled beatifically then continued. "As I expected, Papa wanted to know the names of the culprits so he could go and horsewhip them."

Orlando entirely sympathised with that viewpoint. He'd felt the same when first told.

"I wouldn't tell him—I didn't want to become part of a national scandal. He finally settled for making sure no boys in the family were ever sent to that particular school again. Any road up, as the footman has the endearing habit of saying, I felt so relieved and happy that I found myself telling them about Richard."

Orlando remembered with great fondness the afternoon Jonty had told *him* about his first love and the lovemaking which had ensued. "Whatever did they say?"

"You must remember I hadn't planned to say anything at all—they'd never even met the lad. It just all got blurted out accidentally, and what a shock it was to the three of us. Mother cried once more—she must have to use sails for handkerchiefs—but Papa—" Jonty smiled again, with real pride. "Papa was a revelation. I'd thought, as soon as I realised what I was doing, that I'd made a dreadful mistake. He is such a moral man, Orlando. He's always drummed the Ten Commandments into us, going on and on about the sanctity of the marriage vows." He grinned. "You should hear what he says about the morals of His Majesty. In private of course, he's not daft. To my great astonishment, he launched into a series of disclosures himself. It seems he'd advised Oscar Wilde to flee the country when the scandal about Bosie first broke."

Orlando shuddered. "Not Wilde again. I really don't think I want to hear anything more about that man."

Jonty grinned at his lover's discomfort. "Well, hear you shall. It appears Papa even offered to pay the man's fare to the continent, although whether that was out of sympathy for him or a desire to get one over on the Marquess of Queensberry or his 'hideous whelps'—Papa's words, not mine—I never established. Anyway, after much digression on the subject of hypocrites and people who should know better, he's a terrible one for going off the point, my father..."

"Not something *you* ever do, is it? Ow." Orlando was given a swat for his pains.

"His main concern seemed to be that I shouldn't lay myself open for blackmail. He recommended discretion, a single partner to whom I would be loyal and no going around looking for 'boys, the downfall of many an honest man, Jonty my son'." Jonty broke into an uncanny impression of his father. "No breaking the Ten Commandments, either. I've been pretty good on most of those points so he's had no complaints. I reassured him that Richard was my first love, and probably my last, which is why I think they both got a bit of a shock when you appeared. They'd thought that their youngest and handsomest son had taken a vow of chastity, thereby breaking the hearts of the entire eligible female populace of London. I daresay some of the male hearts with them." Jonty finished with a huge grin, earning himself a whack on his backside from his second and only love.

"What did they say when you told them about me? About us?"

"Mama squeezed my cheek, said that she thought you were a lovely lad and Papa slapped my back. He said he felt confident that my heart was placed in the safest hands. They didn't bat the proverbial eyelid, either of them."

"I don't know whether I'll ever have the nerve to face them again. They know, and when they look at me, I'll die."

"You are such a melodramatic idiot. You should have taken to the stage, then you could have swooned all over *East Lynne*. They *haven't* treated you any differently, have they? You talked to Mama quite happily all the way home from the racing. I remember her interrogating you about whether I was eating enough because she thought I looked thin."

"I suppose so." Orlando decided he would need to think this one through before they resumed the discussion. They lay in silence for a while, enjoying the last of the sun before it went behind the tall trees up on the cliff. To his great satisfaction, they'd dried off sufficiently to be able to put their day clothes back on over their costumes, assuming instant respectability. They strolled back to the Beaulieu, the bag full of empty bottles and wet towels, yet not a single jellyfish or specimen of a lizard to frighten the ladies with.

Orlando and Jonty spotted Mr. Wilson as they crossed the gardens. It was no surprise when he beckoned them over. "Pleasant swim, gentlemen?"

They simply nodded in reply. They didn't ask how he knew. The inspector seemed to be able to pick up all sorts of things just by observing then putting two and two together. Usually he made four, although in the case of the St. Bride's murders he'd failed to even make three.

"We've been looking at Mr. Ainslie's business affairs. Unfortunately they're as pure as the driven snow, although I think that's more likely due to the influence of his son. Bit of a fly boy, our Charles Ainslie."

"So we understand. Mr. Sheringham told us at length."

Wilson raised an eyebrow "So you took my hint, gentlemen? Though which of you is Mr. Holmes and which is Dr. Watson I've yet to fathom out. I hope that you'll be sharing the fruits of your labours with us?"

Jonty grinned. "Of course we will, Inspector. I'll make a full written report at the end of the day. Or Dr. Coppersmith can and I'll correct his spellings. Please excuse us just now, I can see the next victims for our powers of interrogation." He nodded towards the "Misses". "They can't fail to fall for my colleague's considerable charms. I bet we can persuade them to tell us more about their fathers' businesses, and any connection there may be to the dead man, than they'd ever reveal to you." He grabbed Orlando's arm to drag him off in the direction of the terrace where the young ladies were taking tea.

"Jonty," hissed Orlando, "we're not going to talk to them, are we?"

"Even Sherlock Holmes wasn't above a little flirtation to suit his ends. We won't flirt, well, not very much. You can just look serious and ask penetrating questions. You'll like that." They bounded along the terrace, Jonty positively beaming at the girls. "Good afternoon, ladies. May we?" He indicated one of the vacant seats at the table, then elegantly placed his bottom on it, motioning Orlando to do the same.

"Did you have any luck with your scysophoa or whatever it was?" Miss Sheringham, the bolder of the two, enquired.

"Alas no, they avoided our grasps unceasingly. Even the Reptilia who sported themselves in the sunshine wouldn't let themselves be taken. Would they, Dr. Coppersmith?"

"Indeed not. Shall I pour you another cup, Miss Sheringham?"

Jonty was surprised at his friend's forwardness. *Oh, well done, you, rising to the task at last.* If only he could maintain his naturally reserved look, employing those big brown eyes, these girls would be eating out of his hands. In no time he'd wheedle out of them all the information they knew about the Ainslie family. Jonty suppressed a chuckle, thinking about how the girls might have reacted if they'd seen his lover just a few hours earlier, dripping wet in his swimming costume. *They'd have probably fainted. I nearly did.*

The general chit-chat progressed from the doings of the day to the murder of the Monday afternoon. Much feminine sympathy for the handsome Mr. Ainslie was forthcoming. "Such a lovely young man," gushed Miss Forbes, fluttering her eyelashes at what she no doubt regarded as two gorgeous creatures gracing her table. "Such a tragedy for him. He's taken it so very bravely. He's terribly shy, though."

Orlando rolled his eyes at Jonty. *Very shy, my aspidistra,* the look implied.

"I believe your father knows him through his business?" Orlando turned his charm on Miss Forbes, earning him a slightly huffy look from Miss Sheringham.

"Oh, yes. There's quite a rivalry over some aspects of the business, although they each have their specialities." Miss Forbes poured Jonty another cup of tea, earning herself another glare from her pal. Jonty wondered whether they saw themselves as rivals for his attentions. Or Orlando's. Or any eligible young men who might come their way. "Father had quite a lot to say when he discovered we were both staying here, not much of it complimentary, although not to young Mr. Ainslie, only to his father. I really daren't repeat some of the things he said."

Miss Sheringham snorted. Jonty suspected that she wanted to reclaim control of the conversation and turn attention back to herself. Girls really could be very trying at times. "Well, *my* father could tell you rumours about young Mr. Ainslie, not just his father." Both pairs of male eyes fixed on her.

Jonty tried to appear at his most arch; this was becoming an amusing game. "Now, you're not going to indulge us in the same tittle-tattle, are you?"

Much feminine giggling. "Well, it was after I was asked by Mr. Ainslie to walk down to the harbour with him. We admired the boats." She cast a small glance at her friend, who looked like she was silently fuming because she'd never been invited to walk anywhere, by any of the eligible males in the vicinity. "Papa was furious when he found out. Said he'd just heard a thing or two about young Mr. Ainslie in a letter he'd received that morning. He said I wasn't to associate with him anymore."

"Hasn't stopped you flirting with him when Papa's not around, though, has it?" The waspish tone in Miss Forbes voice was noticeable and her friend had the grace to blush.

"Do you know what this letter said?" Orlando tried to produce a winning smile, very nearly succeeding.

"Oh, no. It was just something scandalous. He said it hadn't been substantiated at all, although if it was, there would be hell to pay. Oh, don't look so shocked, Mavis, I'm quoting his very words, not mine."

There appeared to be little to be gained by continuing the discussion, especially as the girls seemed to be at daggers drawn, so the young men made their goodbyes, pleading that they had to tidy up before dinner.

At the meal, Ainslie wasn't present. "Dining in his room," the manager told Mrs. Tattersall, who had of course enquired.

"Hope he's eating as good a piece of pork as we are, Orlando." Jonty was stuffing his face with crackling and apple sauce.

"I don't know where you put it all. You should be the size of a house by now, the amount you seem to get through."

"Burn it all off, old man. My mother says it's nervous energy. Although they do say she was a tiny little thing in her youth, and I hope I haven't got a shock coming."

As Orlando laughed, most of the conversation in the restaurant ceased. No one had seen this serious young man laugh in the six days he'd been there. The occasional smile, yes, but never so much as a giggle otherwise. Two couples had even taken up a little side bet as to whether he'd ever seen the funny side of anything. Now he was laughing, his stern face became extremely handsome. If he didn't notice their looks, Jonty did, and felt very proud to be able to produce such an astounding effect in his friend.

📖

Dinner finished, coffee drunk, a lighthearted game of rummy, then off to their suite. Jonty picked up the Beaulieu's guide to its facilities and thumbed through it. "There's a dance every Friday night, Orlando—we must go to the one tomorrow." He waited for his friend to react as though he'd just said *there's a hanging every Friday night, Orlando, we must go to the one tomorrow.* He wasn't disappointed. "You can dance, I take it?"

"I had lessons when I was younger. I was actually quite good, although I'm rusty. Still, the basic principles are mathematical so I should soon pick them up again." Orlando looked very dignified and Jonty wanted to pinch him. Or seduce him.

"I bet you don't actually *want* to dance, do you?" Jonty received a shake of the head in reply. "Well, you'll just have to bite the bullet. It's your duty, given that there are only three eligible men in the hotel and I don't think Matthew Ainslie is up to dancing yet, even if it were the done thing."

"Who, dare I ask, will you take the floor with?"

"I'll dance with Mrs. Tattersall at least three times and each of the young spinsters twice. Once would be insulting among so small a company of unmarried people yet three times might occasion talk. I haven't decided whether I'll ask the blushing bride to dance, not wishing to arouse jealously in the equally blushing groom's bosom." Jonty grinned. "I think *he's* the murderer. He found out that Charles Ainslie was intending to take his lady wife up into the woods to see the honey buzzards so had at him with a meat skewer."

Orlando frowned. "How can you make jokes about murder, Jonty? After last time?"

"It's precisely because of what happened last time that I feel the need to joke, Orlando. Gallows humour you could call it. Very well, it might be. I'd rather laugh than cry any day so I'll enjoy myself thoroughly at that dance. I want every woman in that ballroom to see you looking gorgeous and wish that you were taking her up to your room—I'm ignoring that blush because I think you've learned how to fake them. I want to stand there smug in the knowledge that *I'm* the one you'll be sleeping with tomorrow night."

As Jonty smiled, Orlando noticed for the first time the finest of lines on the skin coming down from his friend's eyes. They added a gravity to his appearance which made him even more desirable. He took him in his arms. "I want to stand in the ballroom and have every woman fall in love with you. I can picture going up to each of them and saying, "Dr. Stewart isn't available, ma'am, Dr. Stewart wouldn't kiss you for all the tea in China, miss, Dr. Stewart will be sharing my bed tonight, madam." I want to imagine the shock on their faces."

Orlando pulled Jonty's face close and kissed him passionately, more inflamed by the outpourings of these stupid imaginings than he cared to admit. This fantasy about confessing his love to total strangers was ridiculously arousing. He'd just started to undo his lover's shirt buttons when a knock on the door made them both jump. Their hands moved like lightning to adjust their dress to something like propriety before they dared turn the lock.

It was the hotel manager, pale and anxious. "I'm sorry to disturb you, gentlemen. I wonder whether you could be of assistance? I know, Dr. Stewart, that you've been friendly with Mr. Ainslie so I was rather hoping you would come with us and talk to him."

"We'd be glad to oblige." Jonty adjusted his tie. "What's this about?"

"I rather think—" Greenwood raised his hand to forestall Orlando, "—that this calls for only one of you. It's a very delicate matter." The manager looked around, lowering his voice another notch. "I don't think he presents any danger to anyone except himself. It appears that he's threatening to take his own life."

Chapter Six

As Mr. Greenwood accompanied Jonty along the plush carpeted corridors of the Beaulieu, he explained the situation as he understood it. Matthew had taken his dinner in his room. One of the waiters, coming to take away the empty dishes, had found the man with a half empty bottle of whisky at his side and a revolver next to it. When Greenwood had gone up to investigate for himself, the bottle had been slightly less full, and the revolver was being swung around in the air. The manager didn't lack bravery; he'd calmly suggested that Matthew put the gun down and be sensible.

"You are in no danger from me, my good man," Matthew had insisted. "There's only one intended recipient for this bullet. Me. When I've drunk enough to give me the courage."

All this had been spoken with the strange dignity of the truly inebriated, or so Greenwood reported to Jonty. "I had to fetch you, Dr. Stewart. The only alternative would have been Mrs. Tattersall, except I was afraid that the shock of the gun might kill her."

Jonty wondered whether the manager was speculating if a heart attack would be even worse for trade than suicide. He hadn't felt particularly afraid, even before Greenwood's reassuring words, although he was racked with guilt about having left Orlando behind in their suite to fret. The man had insisted he be allowed to come along, but Greenwood had been equally insistent that only one person was needed.

Jonty once more found himself knocking on the door of Matthew's room. "Matthew—Mr. Ainslie—it's Dr. Stewart. Can you spare me a moment?"

There was a sound like a chair being knocked over. The door opened. "Jonty. I'm afraid that I'm unable to attend you tonight. A bit preoccupied." The drink couldn't obscure the dignity in Matthew's voice.

"That's quite alright, Matthew, I just wanted to check you were quite well. Been a hard few days, hasn't it?" Jonty slowly started to inveigle himself into the room.

"It has that." Matthew let go of the door, allowing the other man to enter. Greenwood stayed discreetly aloof. Jonty eyed the bottle—it was almost empty now—then surreptitiously looked for the revolver. With a sickening feeling in the pit of his stomach, he saw it in Matthew's hand.

The man might have been inebriated, but he seemed quick to notice the look on Jonty's face. "Don't let this thing worry you. Only intended for my own use." He politely indicated a chair.

Jonty wondered why ridiculously well-mannered madmen made a beeline for him. Only Matthew didn't seem mad, not like the St. Bride's murderer had been, just sad and confused.

"I would offer you a drink but there's not much left. I'm afraid your visit will have to be a short one, unless you want to see me kill myself?"

"I've seen a man kill himself before, Matthew." Jonty's words were a chilling echo of Orlando's back in the times of the college murders. "Not a pleasant thing by any means, such heartbreak for the family. I remember the young lad's mother being so determined not to cry when they came to visit the college."

"I have no close family now, Jonty. There were only the two

of us. I've no female relatives to come and weep either with me or over me."

Jonty tried another tack. "What about your business? They must rely upon you, especially now when there'll be so many responsibilities. You can't let them down."

"Why not? I've been let down many times over the last few years and left to get on with things. Perhaps they should have their turn." Matthew reached for the bottle but Jonty had neatly edged it out of reach.

"What is this all about, Matthew? Why the gun?" There was no point in prevaricating; the man had to be talked out of or into using the weapon, or else they would be sitting here till kingdom come.

Matthew looked carefully at his guest, considering. "My father has—had—long wanted me to marry, produce an heir for his business. I've avoided it for what I think will be obvious reasons to you." He looked up, acknowledging Jonty's slight nod of assent. "I think you'll have guessed by now that my tastes are not those of every man. I've managed to serve them well, with discretion, throughout my life. I've also managed to keep them a secret from my father, or had, until two months ago. How he found out, I don't know—I suspect he might have had me followed. Anyway, his discovery was followed by an ultimatum. I was to find a girl, woo her and wed her, all within the next six months. I was given the dispensation of a longer period to produce the required grandchild." Matthew flashed an unexpected smile.

Jonty felt that some sort of reply was in order, though he was pushed to know what would be helpful. Matthew had suddenly confessed to a wonderful motive for murdering his father and an equally good one for killing the person to whom he'd just revealed it. That gun looked horribly threatening. "I'm always grateful that I'm one of a brood, with no requirements of lineage upon me." It was the second time in as many days that

Jonty had listened to a story of parental pressure, of being expected to conform when that act was against all one's needs and hopes. He would thank God again this night for his own parents.

"I'd decided to ask one of the unattached young ladies here to oblige me. I guess that I'm no great catch, yet they seemed to be amenable to letting me woo them. It would have been an unhappy match for me—any match would. I'd have made some endeavour to be a good husband and I'd have tried to produce an heir. Now it isn't necessary." Matthew sighed, fiddling with the gun.

"Then I don't see why you feel the need to take your life. I could understand if the pressure to do what you didn't want to had driven you to suicide. But the requirement to conform to someone else's expectations is no longer there."

"The knowledge of my own nature remains, Jonty, and the fact that I tried to force myself upon your friend. That was a grave error of judgment, which I've got away with lightly so far. A repeat of such an incident might bring scandal or worse. I don't want to end up with two years' hard labour."

Jonty was trying to weigh up whether he could grab hold of the gun, eventually deciding it wasn't worth the risk. "I must admit I was surprised that a sensible man such as you should have acted quite so precipitately. You hardly know Orlando."

Matthew smiled again, ruefully. "When you ask a man if he understands the true connotation of a book like *The Picture of Dorian Grey* and he says it's one of the things he would very much like to find out, then you've an inkling that he might be sympathetic to your inclinations. I was wrong to act on such small signs. My only excuse is that factors have conspired to drive me to be less than sensible, almost as if I've had to make the utmost of my last chances of freedom."

Jonty nodded. He also made a mental note that he was really going to have to teach Orlando exactly what he mustn't say or do around other people. Probably word for word, like a child. "You have that freedom back now, Matthew."

"I think not, Jonty. Even if my father's gone, there's just the little matter of this." He reached over to the dressing table and produced a letter, carefully passing it over to his guest.

Jonty could hazard a guess at its contents before he had even read it—the merest skim through vindicated his assumptions. Blackmail. The one thing that his own father had been so frightened of for his son. A simple threat to "tell all" unless a certain amount of money was placed in the sender's hands by the usual complicated type of route.

"When did you get this?"

"The day after we reached here. I've been worried sick about it, unable to take any action other than reply to the address of convenience that's given, pleading for some more time because I can't access sufficient funds until I'm back home. I received a reply yesterday." He produced another letter, which he read out loud, his tones decidedly more sober now. The threats were still there, termed in even coarser language, the stake had been raised, but the time scale had extended until the start of September, which would be just after he was due to return home.

"Do the authorities know about this?"

Matthew laughed bitterly. "Should I show them it? Ensure that I was straight on the road to jail? I don't know how Jersey law stands, but Wilson is from the mainland and he'd have no truck with *pederasts* or whatever vile term he'd use for fellows like me. I've known men destroyed by blackmail. Frankly, I'd rather take an easier route to my destruction." He waved the gun again.

"Matthew, would you put that bloody thing down. You're not going to kill yourself. You're going to fight this evil bastard." Jonty waved the letters. "And we're going to help you. The inspector is a man of enormous discretion and common sense, the university wouldn't use him if he weren't. My family isn't without a little influence, they can wield a bit of clout should we need it. You can't let this person conquer you, Matthew, he just isn't worth it." Jonty stretched out his hand. "Give me the gun, now. I don't want to see you hurt for the sake of some twisted individual."

Matthew considered. "Can't see the point. I'll end up just paying this swine until he gets fed up with bleeding me dry, or waiting for the police to arrest me. No life in either."

Jonty sighed. "Then you'd better just shoot yourself, because with that attitude there'd be no point living."

Matthew seemed totally surprised. He looked at Jonty, looked at the gun, then simply handed it over. Whether Jonty had finally persuaded the man that he was being an idiot or whether he'd somehow struck a strange chord among the drunken logic he couldn't tell, but he gratefully received the weapon and gingerly opened the chamber. It was empty.

Jonty was exasperated. "Matthew, you've put me through all sorts of hell here, then it turns out this bloody thing isn't even loaded!"

Matthew looked sheepish; he fumbled in his pockets, bringing out a pair of bullets. "Must have forgotten."

"You are an idiot. Now I think you should get into bed and try to sleep. You're going to have a stinker of a head in the morning, which won't help when we see the police." Jonty rose. "My own experience tells me that life is rarely easy. I've faced many a challenge, too, but they each have to be fought, or else evil will win every time." Having delivered his sermon, he took his leave.

📖

"I don't know if decadence has heights or depths, Orlando. Whatever it has, we're at them." Jonty smeared his toast with a thick helping of Jersey butter, then crunched into it. Breakfast in bed—they hadn't had such a luxury since they'd been in the sick bay after the St. Bride's murders. The atmosphere then, and Nurse Hatfield's frighteningly starched pinny, with equally starched bosom behind it, had rather spoiled their enjoyment.

Now, sitting together in a double bed, trays on their laps laden with tea, toast and an array of cooked delights, this was indeed another foretaste of heaven. Mr. Greenwood had been extremely grateful for Jonty's endeavours the night before, not least because it kept scandal away from the hotel. A murder they could cope with, but suicide would be a disaster to trade. So a late breakfast in the privacy of their own suite was the least he could do to express that gratitude.

Such a breakfast, as Jonty kept saying. No bacon or sausages today, although the Beaulieu's butcher must be a man to be valued as his meat had been consistently excellent. This day it was scrambled eggs, light as a cloud, topped with smoked salmon and a tiny spoonful of caviar. Jonty ate as if he hadn't seen food for years.

He'd returned to their suite to find Orlando in his pyjamas, asleep on the sofa, looking worn out. Kissing him gently on the brow, with a murmured, "Back now and all safe," he'd flung himself on his own bed without removing more than his tie.

So the libations of butter and egg with which he was anointing himself were dripping onto his shirt, not his best silk jim-jams. The hotel laundry would have to deal with it, like all the rest of their stuff.

"I was very worried about you, Jonty." Orlando looked very young, charmingly vulnerable.

"But Greenwood assured us he believed that Matthew was no harm to anyone except himself. He said that before I left our suite—I might have had second thoughts, if not."

"He couldn't be sure. A gun is an even more dangerous thing than a razor."

"Not when it has no bullets." Jonty chuckled at the thought of Matthew's blank expression and the sheepish one which rapidly followed.

"You didn't know it wasn't loaded. Not till the end. You shouldn't have gone."

"So I should have let a poor unhappy man kill himself?"

"You said yourself the gun wasn't loaded." Orlando grimaced, fiddling with his toast.

"Don't quibble. Anyway, we didn't know that at the time, which is an argument you just used on me. Are you losing your rational powers under the strain of this, Orlando?" Jonty produced a grin at his friend's evident discomfort. "Anyway, if he'd remembered the bullets, my conscience would have had to live with a man's brains being splattered all over the wall. Had to do the right thing, old chap. Each of us has to recognise his responsibility and fulfil it."

"What would it take for you to stop putting yourself into danger? Would I have to beg you?" Orlando looked as if he was going to cry.

"Ass." Jonty took his lover's face tenderly in his hands, delivering an eggy and salmony kiss.

"I mean it, Jonty. I would do anything, give you whatever you asked, if you were just to promise me that you wouldn't be so devil-may-care."

"What would you grant me, Orlando, my lord? Up to half thy kingdom? Mama says my smile could wheedle three quarters of a kingdom from any monarch."

"You have my whole life. What more could you want?"

"Would you answer me any question that I asked you, without reservation?" Jonty cocked his head to one side.

"If it were in my power to do so, yes."

"Why did your father cut his throat?"

Orlando winced as if he'd been kicked in the stomach.

Jonty grabbed his hand. "I don't ask this idly, believe me. It's preyed on my mind this last six months—I can take it no longer. That talk with Matthew has brought it uppermost in my thoughts. Please tell me, I implore you." When his friend remained unmoved he played his last card. "Do I have to get down on my knees and beg, Orlando? Because I will." He rose from the bed, lowering himself to the floor.

Orlando leapt up, dragging him back to his rightful place. "You will never beg me for anything, Jonty. I'd lay myself completely open to you before I let you abase yourself." He sighed deeply. "I'll tell you everything." There was a long pause before he recommenced. "My father wasn't a well man. He suffered terrible bouts of what I guess the clever folk would call a depressive state or some such term. He would reach such depths. I would see him sitting with his 'black crows' about him, as he would call it afterwards, when he was more himself. There are times when I think I've been dogged by those same crows myself. But not these last ten months."

Jonty couldn't resist a smile, and Orlando almost managed one himself. He carried on. "I suppose things got so dark for him he couldn't see a way to carry on. He was crying *that* day. You know, I had never seen him cry before. We were in the parlour having luncheon. He took the carving knife then said, 'I hope you know that I have a great fondness for you both—goodbye.' After that..."

Jonty brought out his handkerchief to mop the tears which were flowing along his lover's cheeks. "Shouldn't have asked you, old man. Unfair. Sorry."

Orlando sniffed, blowing into his own hankie. "No, it's all right. It's been a relief to tell you at last." He looked straight into

Jonty's eyes and produced the most relaxed smile he'd ever seen on his face. "No secrets now, not one. Clean slate."

Jonty caressed his shoulder. "Come on, finish your breakfast. What would my mother say if she saw how lean you are? 'Jonathan, you're neglecting that young friend of yours. He needs at least six square meals a day and a very hearty breakfast.' Only I think she might well say 'that *young man* of yours' because she regards you in the same light as her other son-in-law. In fact she likes you a sight better."

Orlando smiled, displaying the affection he had for Mrs. Stewart, particularly now that she didn't frighten him sick any more. He picked up his toast and nibbled at it. "So where are we, Jonty? A man's been murdered. We know pretty well how, so there seems little point in speculating as to the weapon employed. Very few people can have an alibi for the time—well, snort if you wish, Mr. I-don't-trust-alibis-at-all, but at least they can eliminate people from suspicion. Unless they drug their friends into supplying them," he added hastily.

"Have to start with *why*, Orlando. And who he'd trust to be in the room with him alone."

"His son."

"Too obvious and out of all keeping with what I've seen of him." Jonty raised his hand to stem the imminent anti-Ainslie flow. "Begin elsewhere."

Orlando frowned. "We should remember the last time. Start with the most unlikely person."

Jonty giggled. "That would be you, I think, my dear. Got so cheesed off with the honey buzzards incident you went straight off to take revenge on the old man. You told him you were a phrenologist and wanted to read his bumps. Round the back, then Bob's your uncle!"

Orlando slowly and deliberately took the breakfast trays to put them on the floor. He pulled his lover over, encountering not an ounce of resistance, and whacked his backside. "Idiot, but the idea's sound. Who is the least likely? That young bride, I would say, or Mr. Tattersall."

"And you'll hate me saying this, but Matthew himself doesn't seem very likely to me either. I think if he'd stabbed his father to avoid the unwelcome marriage, he'd have told me last night, then killed himself. He'd not have forgotten the bullets in that case."

"I trust your judgment in this, Jonty, despite my misgivings. So, what now? Look for the blackmailer? I suppose if Ainslie senior knew about the letters he might have decided to confront the writer. He or she must be here, on Jersey, if they were delivered by hand."

"I would love to find out more about *our girlfriends'* fathers. Oh, you can cut out the snorting. It was a joke and you know it was. I wonder what Mr. S had found out that was so shocking?"

"There's the matter of the card sharpery, too. Perhaps someone Charles Ainslie had tricked at the tables had decided to take revenge by digging the dirt on his son." Orlando stretched, yawning greatly. "You'll be taking Matthew to see our friend Wilson this morning?"

"Not sure he'll be in any fit state to see anyone much before this afternoon. I'll leave a message for them both to meet us for a pot of tea—until then the time will be entirely our own. What plans do you have? Will we go to the races?"

Orlando considered. "Are our bathing costumes dry?"

Jonty was astonished. "I believe so. I left them out on the balcony in the evening sun. Why do you ask?"

"Thought we might wander down into that little cove again. Won't need any lunch after this lot—we could swim then try to catch the lizards for a few hours."

"You daft old thing. After days of protesting about it, you actually want to go bathing now?"

98

"Indeed I do, Jonty. I'll take every opportunity of doing so this holiday, I think. If that's agreeable with you?"

Jonty beamed. "Of course it is. I love the sea, and bathing is simply the nicest way to spend a warm day, such as this one is threatening to be." He rose, taking his friend's hand to lead him through their lounge to the glass doors that gave onto their little balcony. "Sun's going to crack the paving stones today, Orlando. You can see the way it's burning off the mist already, it'll be an absolute scorcher. Oh, hell!"

Orlando scarcely had time to say "What's the..." before he was dragged away from the doors and behind a curtain.

"Our female friends have just walked out into the garden. If they look up here they'll get a terrible shock."

Orlando felt sick. He'd forgotten that he was only in his pyjama bottoms and Jonty was in little more than a shirt. They were still holding hands. "We must take care, Jonty. If there's a blackmailer here, we don't want him to be finding himself another set of victims."

"I'm not frightened of any blackmailer. If anyone was stupid enough to try it, they'd have my parents to deal with. You're right about the need for discretion, though. We don't want Mavis and her equally ghastly friend twigging—they'd let all the world know." He grimaced. "Get your costume on then, the sea awaits."

As the cove was just as peaceful as the day before, Orlando decided to disrobe right on the edge of the sand with never a twig between him and the rest of the world. This day the rest of the world consisted of two oystercatchers. When Jonty had followed suit, they wandered down to the water's edge, paddling, splashing and annoying the tiny hermit crabs.

"Not sure I like these fellows, Orlando. Always suspect them of strong-arming other people out of any shells they take a fancy to. My zoological friends try to dissuade me of the notion but I remain unconvinced. Now here's something I like, though." He reached into the water, fishing around a while until he'd got a handful of periwinkles. "When I was a lad, I would fill my pockets with these things. So either Mother or Nurse, or more usually both, would force me to tip them out. If I refused, they'd turn me over, upside down, and shake me until all the little blighters had gone. It was so very unfair, I don't think I've ever got over it."

Orlando kicked out, sending a huge spurt of water in the direction of his friend's buttocks. "I bet you had an idyllic childhood, Jonty, I can't imagine anything else with your family. You have no idea how lucky you were, compared to me."

Jonty stopped trying to coax the winkles to crawl along his hand. "I do know how lucky I was, and it was wrong of me to make light of it. God alone knows how much I would give to turn back the clock, to make your early years as blissful as mine were. My only consolation is that you can enjoy some of my family's affection here and now—well, not here and now exactly, because if Mama *were* here she would be scolding you for being too thin. She'd make you eat scones with clotted cream. Then she'd forbid you to swim because the water's too cold." The pair of them laughed—that's exactly what Mrs. Stewart would do.

"Perhaps your mother would adopt me, Jonty."

"No, thank you. I already have two brothers, which is two too many. Brother, no. Best friend, lover, colleague, fellow detective—those are enough for me. Come on, let's swim out to the rocks and bask like a pair of seals." He plunged into the water, heading for the outcrop at the edge of the bay. Orlando soon caught him up, began to outpace him, reached the rocks first, then waited to help his friend up onto the smooth platform they formed.

They did bask, like lizards in the su[...] dripping from their costumes giving them a [...] was perfect, until Jonty spoke out of the corne[...] know that when someone says, 'Don't look', the[...] people do is to turn around to try and see wha[...] ie being warned about, but if you could restrain yourseli from looking up onto the cliffs, I'd be very much obliged."

Orlando did restrain himself, despite the fact that he was itching to know what was going on. "What is it, Jonty? Inspector Wilson, or worse still, Matthew Ainslie?"

"It's the worst case. We've been discovered by the 'Misses'. They're up on the path and I think they're deliberately observing us."

"What are we to do?" It seemed so unfair. This was their special place, where they could be happy alone. Three times they'd visited and this was the first time Orlando had seen another soul.

"Ignore them. I'm fairly certain they can't descend to the beach. It's a fair old scramble down that path which I think they'd baulk at. The problem will be if they hang around until we need to return to the Beaulieu. We'll be too wet to just put our jackets and trousers back on."

Orlando felt sick. "Those bushes give plenty of cover from the front, but from above there's very little, apart from the trees we lay under last time. A beady eye could probably penetrate them."

"Do you think that they'd want to see us dishabille, then?" Jonty chuckled.

"I shudder to think, truly. I wouldn't put anything past them."

Jonty crinkled his nose in thought. "I've got an idea, Orlando, a very bold one, but then my father has always said

101

cowardliness never won a man anything. He should know. He must have been pretty brave to propose to my mother, as she'd got a bit of a reputation for sending off any men who tried it with a flea in their ear."

"And this audacious plan is?"

"I daren't tell you, as you probably won't let me do it if you know." He stood up, making absolutely sure he didn't look at the ladies, who still remained enjoying the view. "You just keep *them* in sight out of the corner of your eye. If there's no immediate effect you'd better let me know." He started to undo the buttons on the front of his costume.

"Jonty, are you mad? What on earth do you think you're up to? Stop it at once." Orlando made to grab at his friend's hands, but Jonty flapped them away.

"I told you it would make you cross. Just leave me to it and play your part as a scout, I need all my wits about me." When all the buttons were undone, he proceeded to peel the garment off his shoulders. "Any movement yet?"

"There seems to be a distinct fluttering going on up there. How far do you intend to go?"

"As far as it takes, Orlando, with a quick dive into the briny if it goes too far." He removed his arms from the costume then let it fall to fully expose his muscular chest. "Still there?"

"They seem a bit agitated although they're still hovering. You're not..."

"Might have to." Jonty inserted his thumbs into his waistband. "Here goes. We need to frighten them off once and for all with no chance of returning, so if it takes the ultimate sacrifice, so be it." He started to edge the material down.

"Stop! They're on the move." Orlando risked a direct look. "I had no idea they could run so quickly." He laughed. "Just in time to preserve your modesty. Put that costume back on now before it gives me ideas."

Jonty obliged, rebuttoning it until he was the model of propriety. "Close call there. Very near thing." He joined in the giggling. "Did I really nearly expose myself?"

"You did. Promise you'll never do it again, except in the privacy of our own rooms."

"Promise." Jonty sighed. "Now back to the shore, Orlando. I've an appointment with the police."

"It was nearly an appointment to discuss indecent exposure."

Inspector Wilson poured a cup of tea and handed it politely to Matthew. Jonty was left to help himself. Mr. le Tissier had brought a coffee from the bar, while Orlando had disappeared somewhere with his books. They were in the garden of the Beaulieu, with a beech tree providing them with some very welcome shade on such a scorching day.

"Dr. Stewart spoke of something that was worrying you, Mr. Ainslie. I see it's been arranged for us to talk without risk of being overheard, so I might conclude that this is something of a personal nature. Am I correct?"

Matthew nodded, fumbling reluctantly in his pocket. If his whole character was about to be exposed, he couldn't delay the disclosure. "There are letters I received after we arrived here last week, letters that were delivered by hand under the door of our suite. I've assumed they were sent by someone at the hotel. The content of them is odious in the extreme." He handed the papers across to let Wilson read them.

The inspector passed them to le Tissier, who perused each page twice, nodding on several clearly significant occasions, then returned them for Wilson's attention. He only needed one viewing before folding them up and placing them in his pocket.

"Odious indeed. Is there any truth in the accusation?"

If Matthew was surprised at Wilson's forthrightness, Jonty must have felt the same. "Is that a fair question to ask, Inspector?" His face expressed his shock. "We're talking about someone potentially incriminating themselves here."

The two officials both snorted. "I don't know about your position, gentlemen," le Tissier began, "but I regard blackmail, particularly blackmail that may be linked with murder, as being of much more importance than any sexual indiscretion." He faced Matthew, who felt the force of his gaze like a blow. "I can assure you that I won't be taking any official action should these accusations turn out to be verified. I've received no official complaint. I'll make no case."

Matthew took a deep breath, only partly reassured. He'd believe the "no case" part when he saw it. "The substance of the allegations are true. I do prefer the company of men, the particular company of men. However, some of the details given are not accurate and these I'd deny unreservedly. I've never resorted to *paying for boys,* as is alleged, nor have I *kept an establishment.*" He looked to Jonty, who gave him an encouraging nod.

"Do you have any idea who could have sent these?"

"If I did I would have taken my revolver and used it on him, or her, last night, rather than making a botch job of trying to kill myself." Matthew registered the surprise on the constabulary's faces, then turned to Jonty. "You haven't told them?"

"Of course not. Not the done thing at all."

Wilson whistled. "A revolver, eh? I think you'd better let us keep that too, just in case you find out who wrote these vile things. One murder is enough to be dealing with, you know." He smiled kindly, shaking his head as if he were addressing a child. "Can't be taking the law into our own hands. That's why I do appreciate that you've seen fit to share these letters with us. Is there anything else you wish to share as well?"

Matthew slowly shook his head. "I can think of nothing else relevant. As far as I know, my father wasn't aware of these letters—he would have kicked up a hell of a fuss if he had been."

"Was he aware of your *tastes*, as we might term them?"

"He was. Although I hadn't chosen to tell him, he'd somehow found out. I believe he'd taken to having me followed, although it could be that he followed me himself. Not a pleasant thought, but that's how it can be. We don't all share our parents' trust." He glanced sideways at Jonty, who seemed fascinated by his teacup.

"What was his reaction?"

"He wanted me to get married, to give him an heir and me a veneer of respectability. I had agreed to do so." Matthew waited for the next question, feeling relieved when the attention turned to his friend.

"Just forgot to mention the matter of the gun or the suicide attempt?" Wilson smiled ruefully at Jonty.

"I had every intention of making sure it was mentioned here—by Mr. Ainslie himself, preferably. He's had a lot to face up to these last few days without someone blabbing left, right and centre about his affairs. That wouldn't help anyone."

"So you regard talking to us as blabbing?" Le Tissier had a cold edge to his voice which made Matthew's hackles rise. He wasn't alone.

"Of course I don't. Inspector Wilson knows that, and I'd hope he sees fit to verify the fact. I've never hidden anything relevant from the police, either now or before. Likewise I don't indulge in idle gossip."

"Then Mr. Ainslie, will you tell us exactly what happened?"

Matthew related the events of the evening before, as well as he could remember them through the alcoholic haze, Jonty chipping in with the odd point. Only the personal things concerning Orlando stayed unspoken.

"So," Jonty took up the tale, "I believe the tension I told you I noticed between them can be attributed to the pressure his father was driving Mr. Ainslie with. Forced marriage is an awful weight to put on anyone."

"An awful enough thing to make someone kill the person making the demand?"

The full force of le Tissier's question knocked any reply out of Matthew.

Jonty soon came to his rescue, an uncharacteristic ice in his tone. "I don't believe that for one moment. Mr. Ainslie would have made a better fist of killing himself if it were true. I think that nonsense with the gun was entirely due to the letters which now reside in your pocket, fear rather than guilt being the motive." He rose, plainly shaking with anger. "I believe that I've said all I can, gentlemen. Please don't hesitate to contact me if I can be of further assistance—" he turned to Matthew, "—to any of you."

As the policemen watched him go, le Tissier unexpectedly laughed. "Have you entirely eliminated Dr. Stewart as a suspect, Gerald? I would imagine he's a formidable young man, should you get on the wrong side of him."

Wilson chuckled. "I don't doubt it, but I think he would have no reason to kill your father, would he, Mr. Ainslie?"

"Not that I know of. I don't think we've refused to publish some nice little book on John Donne that he's spent hours sweating over."

"I don't think the answer lies with your publishing business. It's been going along quite nicely since you effectively took over the running of it last year. My spies suggest there's little to pursue there now." Le Tissier obviously hadn't forgotten that Matthew hadn't answered his question. "Is it a personal thing?"

"I assure you I didn't kill my father. We may not have seen eye-to-eye but I loved him dearly." The memory of a dozen conversations, ill-tempered or pleasant, ran through Matthew's mind.

"Who else held a grudge, then? This blackmailer? Or someone your father fleeced at the tables? Lord Hardley? What about our academic friends—do they have reason? Let's turn this case on its head. What if *they* share your inclinations and somehow your father found out. Would he have tried a little blackmail of his own? Dr. Stewart has the intelligence to know just where to stick in a blade."

"George!" Wilson's sharp warning reminded his colleague he was in the presence of the victim's son. There were proprieties to be observed, even if they believed the man guilty.

"I'm sorry, Mr. Ainslie."

Matthew no longer had any idea of what was truly proper. He wasn't even sure he cared very much either way. "I can't see Dr. Stewart's weapon of choice as being a stiletto sneakily driven into someone's brain."

"True." Wilson continued to use placatory tones. "He'd be more likely to beat a man to pulp with those fists of his. Have you seen the muscles he has on his arms? Quite extraordinary."

"I knew his mother in her younger days—she's given him both his striking looks and those muscles too." A wistful look crossed le Tissier's face. "She was far above me, you know. I was just a young subaltern and she had a whole raft of the lesser aristocracy at her feet." He broke into a laugh. "Didn't stop me proposing, though."

"You amaze me. What did she say?"

"I have no idea. She laid me out with one great blow—she

107

must have had a punch like James Corbett. She was terribly sweet about it afterwards, sent me flowers and an apology. She sent a firm 'no' as well." He sighed. "I just might have been that lad's father."

While the constabulary thoughts turned to nostalgia, Matthew saw his chance of a hasty escape, excused himself, and left.

Chapter Seven

Jonty lay curled up at his lover's side. He'd huffed all the way back to the room, come in muttering under his breath, plonked himself down in Orlando's lap then started to kiss him. Over and over again, until all the anger had gone. He'd then snuggled his head against his lover's neck, letting Orlando stroke his hair.

"That was most delightful, Jonty. I'm not sure what I did to deserve it."

"It was nothing you did, apart from being adorable, which isn't anything to your credit. It's your breeding accomplished that."

"So why the kisses?"

"Apart from the fact that I love you? Because I had a rough time with the inquisition down there and I wanted someone to be nice to me." He rubbed his nose against Orlando's neck, sighing. "You're usually nice to me, so that's rather convenient." They sat in silence for a while until Jonty became aware of the legs beneath him starting to wriggle. "Have you got ants in your pants?"

"No, I've got an elephant on my lap. You forget sometimes how much you weigh, Mr. Muscles-in-my-spit. If you want me to be able to trip the light fantastic tonight with the assorted ladies of the hotel, then you mustn't crush my legs like this. Your mother thinks I have very elegant limbs and wouldn't want to see them squashed so."

"When did my mama say you had nice legs? I don't remember any such conversation."

"You weren't there. We were talking over tea while you were off looking at your father's print of 'Ranjitsinhji in his pomp', as you described it. She told me how much she'd enjoyed tennis in her youth, how fine the young men had looked in their 'bags'. She said she thought my legs probably would look very nice in white flannels and that all the girls of her youth would have broken their hearts over me."

Jonty sniggered. "She used to say the same to me. Fancy finding out one's own mother is such a hussy." He slipped off Orlando's knees, making himself comfy at the end of the sofa. "Now I'll have to sit here contemplating how to tell Papa that his wife has been chatting up her own son's boyfriend."

Orlando couldn't resist laughing a moment longer. "Imbecile. Idiot. Any other insult beginning with *I*. You are so ridiculously sweet when you pretend to be put out. Curl up there like a good boy while I finish my chapter then I'll give you a nice kiss before we have to get the old boiled shirts on." He reached into his pocket and produced a paper bag. "I'll even give you my last bullseye."

"Why do I have the distinct impression that you're treating me like the family pet?" Jonty spoke petulantly but he took the last sweetie all the same.

"Because I am, my own little rabbit."

"You are extraordinarily soppy today, Orlando."

So saying, Jonty simply shut his eyes for twenty minutes of dozing, the bullseye left to grow stickier every minute in his little paw.

📖

The evening promised much. The small orchestra was very good, everyone present had put on their finery with aplomb, even Jonty and Orlando's shirts had turned out crisper than Nurse Hatfield's fiercely starched pinnies. If the ladies at dinner hadn't all been exceedingly well mannered, then one or two of them might just have drooled into their consommé at the sight of these two dashing young men, especially as Orlando could never quite keep his hair as well controlled as the other chaps, despite quantities of brushing and pomade. The curls seemed to want to free themselves, giving him a raffish air.

It was to the great delight of those same females that these two single gentlemen had attended the dance. Many a feminine bosom was in a high state of anticipation of an invitation to take the floor. Orlando was certainly handsome, his reticence and sternness giving him an allure which many a lady from Girton had found appealing. There had been more than one effort at luring Dr. C out to smell the wallflowers, in an attempt to get behind that maddening reserve. Jonty was strikingly good looking, always seeming to attract the females whenever the men were in mixed company. He was gracious and flirtatious with them all, which raised the ladies' hopes in vain.

Jonty spun Mrs. Tattersall around the floor with an easy smile and a graceful air. The lady must have been a talented dancer in her youth—she still retained a lightness of touch in the foxtrot which belied her years.

Orlando was stuck with Miss Sheringham. It had been impossible to avoid asking someone to have the first dance, especially as Jonty had whizzed over to his elderly friend the minute the band had struck up. Orlando held her awkwardly and their dancing was ungainly; not the fault of either partner, it was the lack of mutual confidence which threw them out of synch. Far worse was the girl's prattling. She droned endlessly about the doings of the day and Orlando was being very careful this time not to just say *yes* or *no* at any random juncture. He'd learned his lesson well.

When the two friends decided to sit out a few dances, much to Orlando's satisfaction, he was able to get a few quiet words in. "I'm glad propriety means Matthew can't show his face, Jonty."

"Are you? Still angry at him? I think he's been a pretty plucky chap."

"You don't need to tell me that, I've personal experience of it."

"Oh, do give it a rest, Orlando. That particular incident is done and over. If you have any serious intention of helping to catch this murderer then I think we should be getting Matthew on our side. I suspect he could wheedle more secrets out of the 'Misses' than either you or I could. Miss Sheringham seems particularly smitten."

"Well, he can let them spy on *him* bathing and see how he likes it."

"Are you going to take umbrage with everyone here?"

Orlando had the grace to colour. "No. No, I'm sorry, Jonty, I know I'm being a real curmudgeon. I do like the Tattersalls, indeed there are several couples who are pleasant. I think I could even like Matthew if he hadn't tried the whole honey buzzards stunt. But the 'spinsters of the parish' I draw the line at."

"Is there anyone else here you like? Anyone in particular? Anyone with dark golden hair, blue eyes and a smile which his mother says makes the darkest day light up?" Jonty grinned, flashing his pretty little white teeth.

"Sounds absolutely delightful. If I meet such a paragon of beauty I'll befriend him straight away."

Jonty giggled, then made a sign for the waiter to replenish their drinks. "Need a bit of Dutch courage before I take the floor with Miss Forbes. You can enjoy a chat with Mrs. T." Dutch courage downed, the men went off in search of their prospective partners.

"Dr. Coppersmith!" Mr. T sat beaming, probably with pride at the accomplishment his wife showed at dancing. Earlier he'd confessed it gave him enormous pleasure to see her in the arms of a handsome young man. It also gave his bad leg a well-deserved rest, so dancing with her was doing them both a favour.

"We were taught to dance as children, my brother and I." Mrs. T seemed caught up in a reverie. "My mother thought it as important as any other accomplishment, to be able to hold your own on the dance floor. That's how I met Mr. Tattersall, back at a rather stuffy ball in the Guildhall. My, the things we did in our youth, Arthur and I—Arthur being my brother, my dear, not Mr. T who is called Aloysius, although he'd rather nobody knew of it."

Orlando smiled, as relaxed in this lady's company as he was tense with the "Misses". "I can imagine you were quite a hit with the gentlemen." He grinned again, thinking what Jonty would say should he hear his lover almost flirting. Although whether it counted as flirting when the recipient of one's attentions was seventy-odd was a moot point.

"Oh, I had my moments. On the floor and at the tables, my parents having brought us up to be proficient at cards, too."

"I could tell that from the first evening we played bridge. They succeeded creditably—rarely have I seen such perceptive play. Is your brother still keen on cards, or dancing?"

"Oh no, duck. Arthur died a while back. He'll be beating St. Peter at a rubber or two now, I dare say." She smiled wistfully. "You remind me of him, you know. Terribly serious."

Orlando blushed and studied his hands. Even seventy-something women could cause embarrassment. "Would you like to dance now? I know that you've promised Dr. Stewart, but he's rather occupied at the moment."

They both looked over to where poor Jonty was trying very hard to politely extricate himself from the grasp of Miss Forbes. "Oh, he is rather, poor lamb. I think that someone should rescue him." Her eyes twinkled. "As it wouldn't be seemly for you to do it, I'll have to oblige." She sailed over the floor like a ship of the line and took Jonty's arm. "I'm so sorry to have to take this man away, my dear. He's promised the next dance to me, and the elderly must be indulged."

They glided onto the floor, leaving behind an indignant Miss Forbes. Jonty whispered, "You just about saved my life there. She was insisting that we go out onto the terrace."

Mrs. Tattersall giggled like a schoolgirl. "I dare say you didn't want to have any truck with that sort of thing." She looked over to Orlando, then back to her dancing partner. "Not with Miss Forbes, anyway."

"You sly old thing, how on earth did you guess?" Jonty had decided long before that he couldn't hide anything from this shrewd woman. She reminded him of his mother, except in physique, and you couldn't keep much a secret from the Honourable Helena Stewart, either.

"Oh, I've seen a bit of life myself, young man. You youngsters think that you invented romance and frivolity, but it's been around as long as Adam. Not all the lads I used to know were interested in the girls—it used to cause such a scandal at times. I believe you should live and let live, as long as the innocent don't get hurt." Her face suddenly became serious. "I hate to see the guiltless suffer."

Jonty shivered, thinking of his schooldays, as he often did when people referred to abuse of the innocent. "Especially children, Mrs. T. I hate to see them wounded."

"Oh, I so agree with you, Dr. Stewart. I have two lovely sons and four adorable grandchildren, a great-grandchild on the way, too. It would break my heart to see anyone bring them to harm. I dare say your mother thinks the same."

"She does indeed, ma'am. She has four children, three grandchildren and the loudest voice in the Home Counties. If she found out that someone had been hurting them, she would be a fearsome protector of her kin." He smiled ruefully at the thought of someone sending the sort of letter to him that had been pushed under Matthew's door. His mother would have found the identity of the sender within days—she had all sorts of contacts, that woman—then he would have been torn apart, limb from limb. Both figuratively and probably literally.

Mrs. Tattersall nodded. "It's a wicked thing that the guilty seem to get away with things so often. It's proof you need, of course, solid proof. People who are willing to stand up and speak the absolute truth. Neither of them very common commodities."

As the dance came to an end, they made their way back to the little table where Mr. T was sitting trying to look inconspicuous and as little like an Aloysius as possible.

Mrs. T leaned over to whisper in her young acquaintance's ear. "If you want to sneak out onto the terrace with your friend, I don't think anyone would notice. I'll get Mr. T to ask Miss Forbes to dance, and Miss Sheringham seems to be entangled with that young newlywed, much to his wife's disapproval, if I'm not mistaken."

Jonty nodded happily, then sidled up to Orlando, who was lurking in a corner. "Fancy taking a turn outside? I have a mind for a cigar." Jonty took the occasional smoke although he knew his lover didn't care to see him indulge. He alleged it made his lips taste strange. On this occasion Orlando simply nodded, no doubt happy to get out of range of the "Misses".

The terrace was pleasantly cool. After a turn or two they decided to amble over the lawn to the little fountain, where they could perch on the edge of the bowl and chat without fear of

115

being overheard. Jonty rustled in his pockets.

Orlando sighed. "Must you? I know you rarely indulge, but tonight it would be so pleasant were you not to." There was something in his voice which made all sorts of implications as to what might happen should Jonty's breath remain unsullied.

He gave a soft answering chuckle. "As you wish, Orlando. Just let me light one for form's sake so we appear to have a valid reason to be here." Anyone could have heard the striking of a match against the stones and seen the faint glow as the cigar gently came alight.

"Thank you."

"My pleasure, Orlando. Always like to make you happy."

They sat in silence for a while, until Jonty felt the need to talk. "Do you know the Tattersalls have been married for fifty years? Can you imagine us in our seventies? Your hair would be completely white and I'd be the size of my mother."

Orlando giggled. "Perhaps I'll have to start rationing your Liquorice Allsorts. You'd be Professor of English by then—it would be beneath your station to indulge in them."

Jonty snorted. "You'd be the Mathematics Professor and therefore not allowed even the smallest bullseye, not even on Sundays. It's against university rules, I've read them. English Professors, the same august text states, are expected to live on nothing but truffles and champagne, with fish and chips on special occasions." He laughed. "Do you think we'll still be holidaying together, or will I have got so tired of you I've put poison in your Chelsea buns?"

"I think we'll still be together, growing old and disreputable. We'll be permanent fixtures in the college. No one will dare try to dislodge us." A bright thought appeared to have struck Orlando. "You might even be Master by then. That would be wonderful." His tone suddenly changed. "They wouldn't let me live in the lodge with you, though, would they?"

"Probably not. Don't think the world will become so enlightened so quickly. Could move you into a set of nearby rooms though, then have a secret access constructed. You could sneak in and out at any time, should your arthritic old knees be up to sneaking, or indeed *anything* at that age."

"They're not arthritic now."

Jonty giggled. "No indeed. I saw you tripping quite nicely with Mrs. T, lovely movers, both of you. Shame I couldn't have been your partner." He reached a hand across to squeeze his friend's arm, "Do love you, you know. Don't say it enough."

"You don't need to say it, not in words." Orlando briefly caressed Jonty's fingers. "It'll be the last dance soon. I'll take Mrs. Sheringham if she's up for it, and you ask Mrs. Forbes, that'll wipe the smiles off the faces of their husbands. And their daughters. Then we'll be allowed to make our way up to bed."

"A handsome plan. So to bed, where actions may be given free rein to express what words can scarce dare to hint at."

"That's lovely. Is it Shakespeare?"

"No, it's Stewart, inspired by a theme of Coppersmith. I hear a waltz. Duty first." Jonty made an elaborate salute.

"I hope you don't intend to *do your duty* by the young ladies?"

"You know I only ever *do my duty* by you. If you want, I'm ready to do it tonight."

Orlando was convinced his heart would have leapt out of his chest had he not his best boiled shirt on to contain it. "Then mark your card for the last dance with me, Jonty. To be performed in our suite."

The sound of the orchestra still rang in their ears as they

opened the door to their rooms. Orlando closed it carefully behind him then immediately took his lover in his arms. "I promised you the last dance. We'll have it here and now." They slowly waltzed across the room, Orlando leading them expertly between the little tables and the sofa.

"Why must I be the woman? I'm sure your mathematical noddle would be better at reversing the steps."

"You can lead next time. If your home in Sussex is as spacious as you keep saying it is, there should be ample room for dancing." Orlando drew Jonty close, took in the aroma of his hair, newly washed that afternoon and still smelling of lavender. "If I were a woman, I wouldn't let anyone else dance with you."

"If you were a woman, I'd get my mama to tell you that I'd injured a certain part of my anatomy in a hunting accident, so couldn't be interested." Jonty buried his nose in the folds of his lover's jacket.

"You are such an idiot at times." Orlando kissed the top of his friend's head. "I sometimes wonder if I really do love you, or simply tolerate you in an attempt to keep you from causing chaos amongst the rest of the world."

"I have no idea what you think, Orlando, not being inside that handsome head of yours. But I do know what this means for me and that's pure adoration. Well, perhaps not so pure, the way I feel at the moment. That wretched bed in your bedroom is singing to me, giving me the most impure thoughts." He toyed with his lover's shirt buttons.

"Then let it sing all it wants. Even if I was tone deaf I could follow that song very clearly." Orlando put his arm around his friend's waist, starting up the dance again, the sensuous steps of the waltz leading them into his bedroom. As they reached the bed, he gently pushed the man onto it, kneeling by his side, pinning down his arms to better smother him with kisses.

"Very masterful, Orlando." Jonty broke the fourth kiss and

came up for air. "I think being dominant suits you, taking the lead and all that."

"I like being masterful." Orlando remembered the first night of the holiday, when he'd felt so protective. How wonderful the sensation of caring for his lover had been. "You don't mind, do you?"

Jonty, as he had the annoying habit of doing at the most sensitive moments, got a fit of the giggles. "Just as well you weren't born a Viking, isn't it? Or one of the Mongol horde. Fat load of use you'd have been at the old rapine and pillaging. *You don't mind if I steal your sheep, do you?* Of course I don't mind, you great pudding. It's a lovely variation on your usual romantic style."

Orlando wondered if he were the only man in the world to find the term "great pudding" strangely endearing. He laid his fingers to his lover's lips then began to unfasten Jonty's shirt buttons, stroking each inch of skin as it was exposed. Once the entire line was undone, he pushed the crisp white linen back to expose his magnificent chest. It hadn't acquired the golden sheen the summer sun had placed on Jonty's face and hands, this flesh always being hidden behind shirt or swimming costume. Its pallor made it gleam in the thin stream of moonlight which pierced the crack between the curtains. Orlando caught his breath once more at the beauty of his lover's body, hastening to express his awe with lips and hands. It seemed ridiculous that Jonty's skin tasted so delightful, a mixture of sweat, soap, even—now they were on holiday—the added element of the sea.

"If this is you being masterful, then you can be so whenever you want." Jonty almost purred, lying back to luxuriate in his lover's attentions.

"I'm not being as masterful as I'd like to be, not yet."

"You can be as masterful as you want." Jonty caressed Orlando's face. "Anything at all, especially what I've always

119

wanted."

Orlando wondered how he could say no again and not have his lover either punch him or go off in a huff. It had come perilously close a few times recently; Jonty was losing patience. It wasn't just the fault of those wretched books, of course, the disgusting ones he'd come across during their first investigation. Although he was happy if that was all Jonty thought had put him off sex.

He decided the only course was diversionary, so started to work on more buttons, the ones below the waistline. More flesh was uncovered, more skin to delight, flesh ready to be taken out and put on parade. "I see you're ready to do your duty for me." He sighed longingly, kissing Jonty's mouth with protracted, fervent kisses.

"I've been ready for that since you started to dance with me." Jonty fingered his lover's curls, seemingly happy for now. "I don't understand how these things work with the female of the species but I can't help feel that every woman you danced with must have been excited in some way. You just have this effect..."

Orlando didn't dare think of what effect he had on women; ignorance would be bliss on this point, so long as they didn't try to lure him into the shrubbery. The only person he'd ever desired was Jonty, and all he wanted to do now was to make his Jonty lose control, to make him squirm until he had the blissful look on his face which only came when they made love. Tonight Orlando would see that look by moonlight and it would almost break his heart in its perfection.

"Come on, then. Let me work my effect on you." He began stroking, fondling, watching his lover's expression all the while, until the moment of climax came and Jonty's face, his eyes screwed tightly shut, shone with exhilaration.

"I do love you, Orlando." Jonty at last found his breath, held his lover tightly. "Please don't dance with any man except me."

"Idiot." Orlando kissed his friend with great affection. "There has been no one but you, there will be no one but you. Now, if you would be so very kind, there's a poor soldier here who wants to do his duty and please could you make it so?"

Chapter Eight

Saturday dawned dry and bright, but it took a long time to penetrate into the skulls of the two young men who occupied one of the beds in one of the Beaulieu's best suites. Orlando eventually woke with a start, leaping immediately from his rest like an old sailor when the drum beat the crew to quarters. He automatically made his way to the other room, arriving with only minutes to spare before the maid brought the tea. Only then did he realise he was in Jonty's bed and had left a blond head peacefully snoring in his own.

Orlando spent a good ten minutes just worrying about whether the maid had noticed and whether she would say anything to her friends. Which then led him to another ten minutes of speculation about how being a servant in a hotel might lead you to having access to all sorts of sources of information that could be tapped into for blackmailing purposes.

Realising his tea had grown cold, untouched in the cup, he ventured across to the other bedroom, where gentle rumblings told him that his friend was still asleep, which at least gave him the satisfaction that he too had missed out on a refreshing brew. But he wasn't to be satisfied; Jonty had obviously woken up, drunk half his tea then gone back to sleep, the little swine. Orlando was so cross that he pulled back the blankets, rolled him onto his stomach and whacked his bottom.

"Ow, stop it. Stop it now." Jonty turned back over, with the pillow in his hands to swat his friend. A swift glance around the room made him realise he wasn't quite where he should be. "Close call, was it?"

Orlando swallowed hard. "Three more minutes' sleep and it would have been two years' hard labour."

Jonty grinned. "That's such a romantic expression to use to your lover in the morning, especially after a night of bliss. I don't know how I cope with the ardour of your speech."

"You'll never really want to take me seriously, will you?"

"No, not if I live to be a hundred. Especially when you pout like that." Jonty stretched. "Unfortunately it seems to be time to get dressed. I have every intention of carrying on the stunning impression we made last night. I'm going to wear my most outrageous blazer, and since you don't have a jacket of sufficient élan to match it, I'm going to lend you a tie that will knock the ladies' hats off."

Orlando grinned, refusing to show the distinct misgivings he had about wearing one of his friend's ties, some of which were particularly *forceful.* "As you wish. I'll happily concede that I did quite enjoy myself at the dance last night, despite my qualms. If you promise that you won't say 'I told you so' or anything like it, I'll state you were right again and that I should trust you much more than I do."

"I won't say it, Orlando. It'll be enough that you'll concede to wearing any tie I choose."

"I agree."

"Good. Because I've brought the red one."

"Except the red one. Any other, I beg you."

"Splendid, seeing as I haven't packed that one at all. It's the orange one I had in mind." As Jonty grinned like a madman, Orlando's only possible reply was a groan.

There was a letter in a familiar hand waiting for Dr. Stewart on his breakfast plate, a letter freshly arrived on the Friday boat. He smiled in recognition of the writing then stuffed the missive into his pocket, having learned at a very early age that communication from the Honourable Mrs. S was best opened in private. They strolled onto the terrace for a postprandial sit down, Jonty immediately beginning to rip at the envelope which was, as usual, tightly sealed. The manager passed, his normal unctuous air already in place for the day, spotted his difficulties and held up a hand.

"I've just the thing for you sir, should you care to use it." He produced a handsome letter opener, holding it hilt forwards, so that his guest could grasp it safely.

Jonty couldn't help noticing how the straight, true blade glinted cruelly in the sunshine, how effectively it opened the cunningly sealed envelope. His mother must have been expecting to have to get this letter unscathed through three rugby scrums and a game of polo for all the security she had applied to it.

At last the stiff, expensive paper began to emerge from its sanctuary, spilling the inevitable reams of gossip concerning the least doings of the least of the Stewarts. There was a smaller envelope as well, with the name *Orlando* impressively imposed upon it, which was passed across for the nominee's perusal.

They read in silence for a while, Jonty producing the odd titter or poking out the tip of his tongue in concentration at the convolutions of life in London and Sussex. "The Manor will be ready for us to visit on the way back to Cambridge, Orlando. Almost all the rooms habitable now—Mama promises not to do anything embarrassing like giving us the honeymoon suite." A big smirk, a quick glance around to see if anyone was within earshot, a look of disappointment that the newlyweds were in the offing, then a stifling of the rather salacious comment he was about to utter.

"That'll be fine, Jonty. I'm looking forward to seeing this country estate that your father has mentioned so often."

"Mother have anything special to say to you?"

"Oh, just the usual. Nothing out of the ordinary." If the awkward words didn't tell Jonty, then the blush should have signalled there was something private within his lover's letter, just as there had been within his own. Neither was ready to share the confidential messages just yet.

I hope that Jonathan is happy, Orlando. Although he has been much happier since he met you than I have ever known him to be. It's not my place to speak of such things, but as you will know by now, I am no great respecter of place or convention, so I will say my piece freely. Look after him. All his life I have wanted my Jonty to have someone who would love him and care for him. He is the most precious to me of all my children, although if you tell him I said that I will brain you next time you grace my doorstep. He's not had the easiest of times; I dare say you know about that, too. Nasty business. Better now. Better with you. The epistle ended abruptly with *your most affectionate friend, Helena.*

Jonty's own letter had contained amongst the tittle-tattle, *I hope that Orlando is behaving himself and not going native. I have always suspected that underneath that solemn exterior, there beats an adventurous heart.* He smirked to think of how those words might have been applied so aptly the night before. *He really is the most dear boy and I profoundly wish that you won't be too cruel to him, as I know how much you enjoy making game of his naivety. The day may well come when he decides he has had enough of it. Then where will you be, my boy? Treasure him and don't take him for granted.*

Once the letters had been read twice, the day needed to be

planned. Shopping was the necessary evil today, but instead of the train or Shank's pony, bicycles were the preferred mode of transport. The pub near the harbour hired them out so a pair of machines had already been booked, Orlando wanting to leave nothing to chance.

"Should we invite Matthew to join us?" Jonty's sweeping arm made a magnanimous gesture. "We could easily find three bikes, and I bet he'd be glad of getting away from the hotel. Those young ladies were making eyes at him across the room all over breakfast."

Orlando sighed. "Not today. Tomorrow, perhaps."

Jonty raised an eyebrow at the encouraging thaw in relations. "Yes, we could walk up the valley after church, maybe find an inn for lunch. Or take the train out to the coast again. See the lighthouse. As long as you promise not to push him over the cliffs. One murder is enough."

"If you were any kind of a friend, you'd say he'd slipped and that I was yards away at the time."

"Daft beggar. I'll catch him before dinner to give him an invite. He might agree to tolerate you for a couple of hours. I'd like to ask him to help us, Orlando. He may well still be le Tissier's number-one suspect, but I think he'd easily get those girls eating out of his hand, the housemaids too if we want. One of those females will have an idea about who's sending these letters. The servants always know exactly what is going on in any household, and a hotel would be no exception."

Orlando started to produce a very small, vestigial glower, then shrugged. "As you wish, Jonty. It can't hurt, especially if he is the culprit—we'll have him close at hand to observe." He rose, stretching. "Now are you going to laze here all morning or are we going to find those bikes?"

"I have no intention of sharing a tandem with you, Dr. Coppersmith. I know exactly what will happen—I'll have to do all the work going uphill, then you'll offer to take the strain coming down the other side."

"Actually my intention was to share the work absolutely, Dr. Stewart. There were no plans for foul play."

"So it'll be just two ordinary pushbikes, then, gentlemen?" The publican was keen to conclude the transaction as he had kegs of beer to attend to that, without question, had a far higher status and importance than these two young Turks.

"Yes, sir." Jonty produced the hire fee, thrusting it into the chap's eager hand. "Don't worry about the change. When do you need these back?"

"Tonight will be fine, if you please, though they're not spoken for till Monday."

The bikes were wheeled out, tyres inspected—they were all in excellent condition—then the deal concluded. The riders mounted their iron-framed steeds, intending to speed off towards the quay, although the word *speed* would be an exaggeration as their progress was wobbly and uncertain as they got used to the bikes. Once they'd reached the road out of St. Aubin, they'd become confident, almost devil-may-care.

Both machines had ample baskets on the front. This had been part of the required specifications, as the whole intention of the visit to St. Helier was to purchase presents. Jonty had two nephews and one niece to provide for, as well as trying to find something for his parents. The children were easy, as any sort of toy or sweets would generally do, although the elder boy liked things that were unusual if not slightly disgusting, like stuffed animals or little packets of joke items. These would need to be scoured for, then selected to provide just the right amount of annoyance to his parents.

Helena and Richard Stewart would be a problem too, as they had everything they could possibly want. So Jonty would usually search high and low for the strange or different or simply amusing, only this time he would have someone to help him. Although how much Orlando could be relied on to offer sensible advice in the matter of shopping was a moot point.

They pressed on as far as the Martello tower then rested for a while to look out to sea. Supplies were being taken out to Elizabeth Castle, the soldiers' voices carrying across the water as they barked instructions. It provided an interesting scene, prompting Orlando to speculate about how the logistics of the operation could be made smoother. Jonty rather switched off, counting the different types of seabird until he realised that the subject had changed from the martial to the commercial.

"I'd like to find something in St. Helier for your mother. She has been so unfailingly kind to me that a present would seem appropriate."

Jonty inclined his head. "I'm sure she'd be delighted. She thinks the world of you, you know. What did you have in mind?"

Orlando looked out at the sparkling sea, face full of uncertainty. "What about some jewellery? I have very little to spend my money on. Apart from you, and you rarely let me pay for anything."

Jonty turned to him, concerned. He'd been left a hatful of money by his grandmother and was far richer than Orlando would ever be. "Does that bother you? Do say if it does. I know I can be a bit overbearing, I get that from Mama. Because I'm always flush with cash, I just want to treat you, that's all." Jonty knew that despite his bold words, their disparity of income rankled a bit with his friend.

"Think I'd like to pull my weight just a bit more, then I would feel less like a kept man." Orlando blushed to the roots of his dark hair.

Jonty didn't know what to say. For once in his life, he was left to resort to his lover's strategy of changing the subject. "We could go halfers on a piece of jewellery. The old girl loves a necklace or brooch and I'm sure there must be a decent jeweller somewhere in town."

"We could buy her a sapphire to match your eyes."

"She already has lots of those. The old man bought them for her in his youth because he was so smitten with her own fair gaze, although I dare say she'd like some more. Something set in silver to go with her hair, perhaps."

"Now what can I buy you? A tiepin? Cufflinks?"

"Think it might be a bit embarrassing to have what I'd like to see engraved on them, Orlando. Let's spend our money on Mama, give her a bit of a treat. I'd like to see her speechless for once when you make your big presentation. She might even kiss you, so keep your hankie handy as she can be a bit sloppy." He smiled to think what Orlando's reaction might be if Mrs. Stewart did attempt one of the big smackers that she usually gave her youngest offspring, leaving him covered in powder and smelling sweetly of her perfume.

"I might just kiss her in return, Jonty, then she'll realise how sad your efforts have been in comparison. A kiss on her cheek from you may well be a familial duty, but one from me will thrill her beyond all reason."

Jonty gaped, gobsmacked. "Orlando Coppersmith! First I find out that Mama has been admiring your legs, now you're offering to kiss her in such a fashion as to turn a respectable matron into a giddy girl. What has come over you?"

"You, idiot. Another glorious night of lying in your arms, listening to your tender words. It would fill any man with supreme self-confidence in his romantic abilities. I remember what you said afterwards—and during. If I believed even half of it, my head would swell beyond being able to get it through the door."

Jonty tittered. "Well, it always seems true at the time. On sober reflection, too. But don't go trying anything on Mama, though. She'd knock you out with one blow if you became too saucy."

"Oh, get on your bike and stop this nonsense. We'll never get even a piece of toffee if you stay here all day chatting." Orlando leapt into the saddle and pedalled away furiously, leaving Jonty temporarily unable to move for laughter.

St. Helier could boast one or two extremely classy establishments. The jeweller's shop they found tucked away in a narrow side street proved to be one of these. They'd begun to despair of finding a gewgaw of the right quality to suit an earl's daughter, despite having been successful in their other endeavours, including rectifying the scandalous situation of Orlando's supplies being dangerously low on bullseyes. There'd even been talk of giving up, settling on buying a hat or, *saints preserve us*, some embroidered hankies, until they spotted a little place which proved to be ideal.

The proprietor looked them over appraisingly, recognised the quality of Jonty's clothes and the insignia on Orlando's cufflinks, then bowed appreciatively. "Good day to you, gentlemen. How can I be of assistance?"

"We're looking for something for my mother. A necklace or a brooch was what we had in mind." Jonty's eyes sparkled as they caught sight of many handsome pieces of work.

"Now, could you enlighten me as to the lady's colouring?" The jeweller held his head on one side, squinting intensively, as though trying to imagine the woman in question through her son.

Orlando spoke up. "You have her glass in front of you, sir. My friend has just the same shade of eye and the hair, if less silvered, is a reasonable match."

The jeweller nodded, squinted again, nodded once more, then turned to a tray. "There are a couple of fine items here, although not new. They came from a family of impeccable reputation, however. The lady of the house would have had a similar colouring to you, sir, if a little paler." He held the tray out for inspection, the jewellery being displayed on black velvet to its best advantage.

"These are very nice—" Jonty eyed them with appreciation, "—but I was hoping for an original, rather like Mama herself."

The proprietor nodded. "I see. Yes. We do have some other things that might fit the bill." He stepped over to a curtain at the back of the shop, "Mr. Renouf, would you please bring out some of the sapphire pieces?" A sandy-haired assistant appeared, bearing another tray, this one full of handsome blue stones adorning platinum settings.

Jonty immediately nodded. "Oh, this is just the stuff."

Orlando nodded too, gingerly picking up one of the delicate earrings. "This little thing is nice, and there's another to match it."

Jonty giggled, caught Mr. Renouf's disapproving eye, hastily stopped. "Well, there would be, Dr. Coppersmith—a pair, don't you know. Actually I think Mama would like these very much. Good choice." He slapped his friend's back. "We'll take these please." His gaze fell on another tray. "Now, I rather fancy this." He pointed to a little tiepin, gold with a single onyx stone.

The jeweller nodded again—the man had begun to resemble a heron—then motioned for his assistant to wrap the two items. Jonty stopped him. "Just the earrings please. The other one will be worn now."

Once outside the shop, Orlando produced half the cost of

the sapphire gewgaws (he'd ensured he'd taken plenty of cash with him, as he didn't want to be seen to be less flush with money than his friend). Jonty carelessly put away the notes and, taking the pin from the pocket where he'd carefully placed it, affixed it to Orlando's tie.

"No, I can't. I thought you'd bought this for yourself."

"Well, I didn't. This is to remind you of your first real holiday and to say thank you for the last few months. Been enormously happy, all in all. I'm not sure that I've told you, really." Jonty reached for his hankie, feeling a sudden need to blow his nose.

Orlando was about to argue again but decided not to. He could see how much this meant to his lover—to force the issue would be unkind and hardhearted. "I should buy something for you, in return."

"No need, really. Smile for me all day. That will be quite enough." Jonty laughed. "Smile for me all day without a single sulk and it will be a miracle."

"You'll at least do me the courtesy of letting me buy you lunch. I'd also like to find a jar of black butter which I can give to your father, just from me. Would that suit?"

"Aye, it would, so long as I get a ride out to the hills before we go home. I have a hankering for a boyhood pastime."

📖

"I used to love rolling down hills as a boy—I shan't ask you if you enjoyed it too, as I can anticipate the answer and it would merely depress me." They'd made their way up one of the many valleys towards the centre of the island, finding acres of rolling sward which rose and fell like great waves over the back of the land.

Orlando contemplated the matter, carefully avoiding

sulking, just as he'd promised. "If it's such a wonderful thing, why don't you do it again? You've had us paddling, collecting shells, annoying crabs, goodness knows what daft things. Rolling down this slope should be meat and drink to you."

"I'm game if you are. We just need to find a bit with no rocks near the bottom." They found an ideal place, all rolling smooth sward with a gently shelving end to the descent. "Now we just lie down, Orlando, then give ourselves a bit of a turn over and..."

Jonty began to revolve down the hill at a frightening pace. When he'd been eleven, this had been the most glorious of activities. Now it was an absolute nightmare. A third of the way down, a descent which seemed to take hours, he decided that he was going to be sick. Halfway down he realised that he was very probably going to die and however would Orlando explain it to his mother? *Very sorry, Mrs. Stewart, but needless to say he was arsing about as usual.* Three quarters of the way down, his life was passing before his eyes, along with newspaper headlines about *Distinguished fellows of Cambridge college found dead on Jersey.* For he was also aware that Orlando's rate of descent outstripped even his and that if he was about to hand in his chips, so was his best friend.

They reached the bottom in an untidy heap. "I thought," remarked Orlando, gasping for breath, "that this was supposed to be a pleasurable activity?"

"It used to be." Jonty's lungs felt like they were ablaze. "Some miserable sod, probably one of your relatives, has come along and turned it into a particularly nasty form of torture." He sat up, immediately regretted it, and lay down again. "Think we should just lie here for a while until we're absolutely sure we aren't going to pass out or away. If anyone comes along, we can say that we're studying cloud formations under field conditions. Under no circumstances should we be interrupted. You can look studious, with a touch of ferocity. I'll smile sweetly, and they'll hopefully depart."

"I'll never do that rolling thing again, Jonty."

"If I even attempt it, Orlando, you must tie me to a tree until the madness passes. Might be time to put away childish things, you know."

"Oh, don't do that to all of them—just the ones that no longer appeal. I enjoyed catching those shrimps, you know, more than anything on holiday. Apart from the swimming."

"More than anything? Really? More than last night when you—"

"More than anything that can be mentioned in broad daylight," Orlando hastily clarified.

"Ah, that's better. Let's just put away the things which have become unpleasant and keep the nice ones. Lying here is quite nice, now that I'm more certain I won't die just at the moment. Ten more minutes, then back to the old hotel, I think."

As they walked through the hotel gardens, they were hailed by a cheery voice. Mrs. Tattersall, in a haze of yellow and white wool, was sitting in the shade trying to make progress on an assortment of little items for the anticipated great-grandchild. She waved the men over and insisted on their drinking tea, sharing a biscuit, then showing her all their purchases. She admired the earrings and the little items found for the smaller Stewarts, but the tiepin was the greatest success.

"Very sharp, these things, you'd better be careful you don't prick yourself with it. Poor Mr. Greenwood was bleeding buckets from his finger after breakfast because he'd decided to reset his tiepin. He gouged the thing into his thumb, silly boy." She shook her head. "Just like these things." She indicated the variety of needles in her workbag. "I never let my little Katie play with any of these, far too sharp. Not dissimilar to those two over there." She inclined her head to where Wilson and le Tissier had just emerged from the hotel, looking rather frustrated.

"We'd better report in." Jonty rose, tipping his hat to Mrs. T.

The officials hadn't been idle, as Wilson carefully explained to his friends. After their discussions with Jonty and Matthew on Friday, logic suggested that Mr. Sheringham had been supplied with some information from the mainland, which had led him to immediately send the obnoxious blackmailing letters. There'd just been enough time for the reply to have gone back via the writer's suggested method—a note to be left in an upturned bucket down by the quay at dusk—and a second letter sent almost by return.

"But not only do I share your mistrust of alibis, Dr. Stewart, I also don't like the obvious." Le Tissier seemed less than convinced by Wilson's conjectures.

"Have you spoken to Mr. Sheringham?" Orlando shared Wilson's distrust of the man, although he couldn't see him as a blackmailer.

"We have. He insists he has nothing to tell." Wilson scratched his head. "He swore he'd received no letters, that he'd said nothing derogatory about young Mr. Ainslie to anyone."

"What did he say when you told him you have an eyewitness to his getting such information?"

"He changed his tune, naturally." Wilson smiled knowingly. "Suddenly he remembered receiving letters about Ainslie, but he was adamant he'd not gone on to issue any threats. He refused at first to produce this correspondence—alleged he'd lost it—but Mr. le Tissier and I ground him down."

Orlando could imagine this formidable pair grinding Stonehenge down. Only Mrs. Stewart would be able to resist them. "Where had they come from, these wretched things?"

"Some source in London." Le Tissier's voice was full of disgust. "They didn't just give a general estimate of Ainslie's inclinations, there were some specific, very nasty allegations as well. They matched those in Ainslie's letters almost word for word. Of course, Sheringham couldn't, or wouldn't, account for the fact that such details could be the same, except to keep denying that he was the blackmailer."

"And?" Jonty sounded belligerent, as if he sought permission to thump the truth out of Sheringham.

"We had to call it a day. We left him in no doubt that he was under extreme suspicion, but we're left with the question, if not him, then who?"

Orlando nodded. "Who else could have got hold of this information? And why should they choose to use it to blackmail Mr. Ainslie?"

"Money, Dr. Coppersmith." Inspector Wilson shrugged, eloquently. "It always comes down to greed in the end, although I'm not sure how this gets us any further forwards. Unless Mr. Ainslie confronted the blackmailer himself and ended up murdered for his pains, yet his son assures me his father knew nothing about the letters."

"What if he did, though?" Orlando felt there was light about to dawn on the case. "What if Matthew told his father about them and they had a blazing row?"

Le Tissier had a keen look in his eye. "He was under enough pressure from his father already. This might have been the last straw."

Jonty's voice, when he at last could get into the conversation, was constrained. "You're wrong, gentlemen. I can't prove it yet, but you are."

Chapter Nine

Sunday morning, Orlando was amazed because church was reasonable again. *Himself* always liked a nice prayer book service but he usually found his own attention wandering. Today there was a visiting preacher who gave a wonderfully intellectual sermon about the true dating of the exodus, which Orlando alone of all the congregation had followed and understood. He made Jonty stand for a quarter of an hour at the lychgate while he quizzed the man on the Egyptian pharaohs.

In the end, he was bodily hauled away by a muttering Jonty with lots of, "Sorry vicar, have another engagement, do excuse my friend's curiosity, mustn't keep you from your lunch."

"What about *my* lunch?" Jonty snapped, as they raced up to the station to meet Matthew, who had gone to Chapel earlier. "My stomach is becoming convinced my throat's been cut and it'll barely last the journey."

Orlando mumbled a reply.

"What was that?" Jonty always became peevish when hungry—this day was no exception.

"I said that you're the very worst sort of exaggerator, if that's the appropriate term. There must be enough meat on you to endure forty days' wandering in the wilderness, so a little extra gap between meals will do you no harm."

It was as well he didn't press Jonty to repeat *his* muttered reply as it consisted mainly of swear words.

📖

Matthew was waiting patiently. Jonty had invited him, when they'd shared a drink before dinner on Saturday, to join them for Sunday lunch. The invitation had been unexpected, but so welcome that even his hosts' poor timekeeping didn't bother him. He accepted Jonty's profuse apologies graciously.

"When Dr. Coppersmith gets the bit between his teeth, he's quite incorrigible, Matthew. It seems that they've decided that Rameses wasn't the pharaoh of the Exodus. Oh no, it turns out he invaded Jerusalem instead, which makes him Shishak. You look just as puzzled as I am."

Orlando opened his mouth as if to carry on some obscure debate; he wasn't allowed to utter a syllable.

"No, you won't bore either of us with this esoteric stuff. You can discuss beer or sandwiches or whether that noise is the train coming or merely the rumbling of my stomach. No Egyptian stuff, please."

Matthew grinned. He liked Jonty, despite the antipathy he'd felt towards him at the start when he only had eyes for Orlando. Jonty had proved unfailingly kind, something Matthew had no right to expect when he'd tried to seduce what he now guessed was the chap's boyfriend. He hadn't spotted their relationship at first, assuming that they were no more than friends, although he'd soon noticed the subtle signs which only those in the know would recognise. Moreover, he was now quite glad that Orlando hadn't given in to the kiss a week ago. Handsome the man might be, but heavens above he was stuffy. How a livewire like Jonty had taken up with him, the angels alone knew.

Still, Matthew was pleased to have something to do for the afternoon, notwithstanding the inevitable awkwardness that remained over both the honey buzzards incident and his suicide attempt. He missed his father—despite the man's faults, he'd been very dear to him. Guilt tinged the grief, the weight of an unwanted marriage lifted from his shoulders replaced by the burden that the last words between them had been part of a quarrel. Sitting in his room at the Beaulieu did nothing to ease the pain.

The train came, they rode down to Corbière, walked up to the little inn up on the cliffs, bought three pints and three crab salads. It took half a glass of beer, not to mention several mouthfuls of seafood, before Jonty had reached a decent mood. Then there was no stopping him. Orlando seemed to have exhausted most of his small talk and was avoiding anything even remotely private.

"Now that the inner man has been, if not satisfied, at least mollified a smidge, I—we—have a suggestion to put to you, Matthew. Would you be interested in joining us in a little amateur sleuthing?"

"I don't quite get your drift, Jonty." Matthew looked from one to the other, unsure of exactly what was being asked of him. It was all highly unusual.

"We've helped the police in the past." Orlando held his glass up to the light, inspecting it as if he thought he would find a murderer hiding among the hops. "There was a series of murders at our college last winter. Inspector Wilson, who took charge of the investigation, asked Jonty and me to help in elucidating some of the germane facts from one or two of our more reticent undergraduates. We were reasonably successful in helping the constabulary to achieve a successful conclusion to their investigation."

"You'll excuse Orlando." Jonty's wry grin spoke volumes. "He tends to use overly long words."

Charlie Cochrane

"I think I followed what was said." Matthew raised an eyebrow. "About this case—as I understood it, you nearly ended up as victims number four and five." It was gratifying to see both his friends' jaws dropping like stones into a well.

Jonty recovered his poise first. "Well, you'd make a fine addition to anyone's detective network. How did you know that?"

"Now gentlemen, apply your own investigative abilities. Who knows everything about everyone at the hotel?" Matthew felt wonderfully smug that the "commercial" had got one up on the "academic".

Two voices spoke in unison. "Mrs. Tattersall."

"Mrs. Tattersall indeed. She has quite a passion for mysteries. She'd read about your college in the *News of the World* and remembered about the story when you came here. She wanted to ask you directly whether you were involved, but the arrival of Wilson made the task easier. She talked to him. He told all."

"All?"

For some reason—Matthew could make an educated guess—Orlando looked as if his stomach was turning over three times. "He said you'd been threatened by the murderer because of your interest in the case." By the expression of relief on Orlando's face, not *all* had been told.

"Wilson has asked us to keep our ears and eyes open again. Would you be inclined to join us?"

Matthew laughed. "Do you think the police would really welcome their chief suspect taking a close interest in the case? Doesn't that take irregularity too far?"

"If you're the chief suspect, I don't think we can be far behind—not if the interrogation I received or the look in le Tissier's eye is anything to go by." Jonty smiled ruefully and drained his glass.

140

"You do know they've searched my rooms? Looking for a tiepin which Miss Forbes saw me wearing and which has now disappeared. I wouldn't be surprised if they've given your rooms the once-over, too."

"Blimey!" Jonty slammed his glass down and earned a dirty look from Orlando. "They didn't tell us that."

"Secrets being kept all round, then." They sat in silence, the drone of conversation from the main bar barely penetrating the lounge.

"That seems to settle it." Orlando's voice was unusually authoritative. "By all of us taking action, we can hasten the pace at which our names are cleared."

The suggestion of being involved in the investigation appealed, not least because it gave Matthew something constructive to do. "So what assignment did you have in mind for me, gentlemen?"

"You've been quite friendly with Miss Sheringham." Jonty grinned.

"Gwendolyn? Indeed. Although you understand what my motives were. Pragmatic, not romantic."

"She doesn't know that, and we suspect she still has rather a hope or two in your direction. She does know, however, that her father received some information about you. We're aware that when the police were questioning him yesterday, they had in mind the possibility of Sheringham being the blackmailer. Orlando thinks that's unlikely, don't you?"

The man in question nodded. "It seems far too obvious. If that were true, he wouldn't have been trumpeting to his family the fact that he'd heard some things to your discredit. Not if he'd any intention of using this information for what is an illegal activity."

"There's some merit in that notion." Matthew shivered at the thought of those letters, of the disgusting allegations.

141

"So, is there anyone else who might have had access to the same stuff? There's always his family, although I find them even less likely in the role of blackmailers than the father."

Jonty chimed in. "Orlando, we've said this before, often. Who always, apart from the Mrs. Tattersalls of this world, knows exactly what's going in any establishment?"

"The staff." Orlando looked as if light had at last dawned in this case.

"Exactly—the staff. I bet someone like Greenwood could glide in and out of anywhere. He'd always have a valid excuse, as would the chambermaids. Matthew, would you know by any chance who 'does' the Sheringhams' rooms?"

"I would indeed. Gwendolyn told me, when we walked down to the quay, that it was a nice coincidence that the same girl attended to both our rooms. Alice, I believe her name is. She's a pretty little thing, if that's your inclination."

"Would it be your inclination to chat to her, Matthew?"

"Such things are rarely done, although they're not unknown." Asking a maid to walk out was nothing compared to the other improprieties he was being accused of. "I dare say I could ask her for a walk on her afternoon off. I believe that's tomorrow, as a different girl turned down the sheets the day..." He stopped, recalling the events of the previous Monday, only a week past but already feeling a lifetime away.

"Tomorrow would be most welcome, if you're up to it, Matthew."

"I'll broach the subject tonight should I see her." He stretched out his sturdy limbs, pushing his chair back from the table. "Now I could do with a walk and some fresh air. Feel like I've been cooped up in that hotel for a month."

"We could walk down to the beach, it was lovely here last week. Orlando will teach you how to catch shrimps, he being a world-renowned expert." Jonty laughed and punched his

142

friend's arm.

When they wandered down to the place where they'd said they'd walked the week before, Orlando stopped, astounded. "Where's the beach gone?"

"You've reckoned without the changing of the tides." Matthew laughed, feeling at ease for the first time in weeks.

"Ah well." Jonty pointed airily up the cliffs. "Let's go and pick hare's-tails to take home for Mama."

"I've met your mother, I believe—that's if she's Helena Stewart." Matthew, like many a man before him, recalled the lady with awe.

Jonty snorted. "I'm not sure there is anyone in London who hasn't heard of my dear mama. Or been shouted at by her. Or boxed around the ears. How did you come across her? I suppose she ran you down in her chariot. Was it the one with the knives on the wheels?"

Matthew felt worried that he'd hit on some tender spot with his new acquaintance, but was reassured when he observed the large smile accompanying all these pronouncements. "No, indeed," he ventured. "It was only the smaller vehicle she uses on Sundays." To his delight Jonty laughed heartily at this response; even Orlando smiled. "My father and she have—had— a mutual friend. Lord Hardley."

"If you will excuse the pun, he's *hardly* the sort of man anyone would be proud to claim friendship with. That business with poor Lady Hardley scandalised society. Mama refused to talk to him after that." Jonty's eyes narrowed. "Said plenty about him though."

Matthew stiffened slightly, tension constricting his voice. "I must insist that, for all his faults, my father had nothing to do with the affair."

Jonty gently laid his hand on Matthew's arm, something Orlando seemed to find annoying. "I know that already. His

143

lordship ran away with the maid, I think most sensible people appreciate that. According to Mama, Lady Hardley wouldn't be able to even spell the word adultery, let alone commit it. She's a poor innocent little thing, so the tale tells."

"It's not just that, Jonty. I know my father had achieved a bit of a reputation for himself with the cards, but he never played fast and loose with the women. He was true to my mother for as long as she lived." The lump in Matthew's throat threatened to unman him. "She adored him, keeping him on the straight and narrow as much as she could. Things deteriorated when she died."

Jonty clapped Matthew on the shoulder then murmured comforting words, two more things that earned him a dirty look from his lover.

📖

The three men walked back to the station pretty much in silence, barely speaking while the train took them to St. Aubin. The appearance of the "Misses" on the road to the hotel sparked them into conversation, most of it along the lines of how they could avoid talking to the girls. Matthew knew a little back path which brought them up into the gardens, a diversion for which the two younger men were very grateful, not wanting to be nabbed this, or indeed any, day.

Back in their room, the fellows of St. Bride's took stock. They now had an ally in the hunt for the murderer, assuming he wasn't the killer himself, something which Orlando wasn't entirely convinced about. The Hardley connection having been eliminated, as Jonty had sworn it would, the identity of the blackmailer seemed the next important thread to unravel.

Orlando's thoughts still nagged him, however, about Ainslie senior's behaviour on the previous Sunday night. Jonty had put the man's agitation down to cheating at cards, but had it really been to do with something else?

"Jonty, a week ago tonight, you thought that Mr. Ainslie was trying to pull a fast one at the tables. Are you sure? In the light of what we now know, given that the man was murdered only a day later, is there anything else that could have cause his erratic behaviour? You said you weren't sure what was going on."

Jonty closed his eyes, trying hard to remember what had occurred that evening. "I remember seeing all sorts of things. Matthew looking at your hands, mainly, and his father getting agitated. You were playing cards, as was Mrs. T, and Mr. T was sitting with me observing the play or at the bar. Hang on a moment, though. Mr. Tattersall was talking to Mr. Sheringham—both Greenwood and the barman were quite close by and could have been listening in, I think. Orlando, I'm astonished. I never realised I would remember all this. It's truly remarkable what one can recall when one really applies the brain."

"Well, apply it a bit more. Did Ainslie senior show any particular reactions to any events around him?"

Jonty poked his tongue out in concentration. "He got a bit annoyed with the "Misses", who were giggling as usual, while eyeing up you and Matthew. There was a lot of feminine gossip going on in their part of the room—I dare say most of it concerned men. Ainslie senior seemed to be concerned with the talk at the bar, too, now you come to mention it. He kept looking over there, I believe, but I could be wrong."

"You rarely are wrong in your observations, Jonty. I should have known that and taken more heed when you warned me about Matthew being interested in me. I was a bit silly then."

"Oh, Orlando, you weren't to know that he was likely to be quite so bold. Although you must take more care in future. As I've said before, you are an exceedingly attractive man and there

145

are bound to be other men who would agree with me. Promise me you won't even speak of Oscar Wilde to anyone except me. Deny all knowledge of him and his works. Say you have no interest in them."

"I will indeed. I'd better not go near the woods or any honey buzzards, either. Nor Matthew." He stopped, considered. "Although you seemed pretty pally with him today."

"Just being friendly. We want him on our side, you know. A little sleuthing may add to the holiday fun, but this seems to be getting a bit nasty, what with threatening letters and all."

"You feel sorry for him, don't you?" Orlando spoke quietly.

"Well, of course I do, the man must be a bit lost at present. Doesn't hurt us to be civil." Jonty was beginning to appear wary, with the merest hint of a frisson in the air.

"You were more than civil this afternoon." Orlando huffed.

"How do you mean?" Jonty's hackles began to rise, just like the great cat he so often seemed to resemble.

"With Matthew. The man who might well have murdered his own father. You were distinctly friendly." The frisson had become a palpable lump of ice.

"In what way?" Jonty was undergoing a freezing of his own.

"You held his arm."

"I did not. I merely laid my hand on it when I wanted to reassure him. Don't snort. I hate it."

"Then you put your arm around his shoulder."

"I didn't do that either, Orlando. You're deliberately exaggerating for some reason of your own. He was upset talking about his mother. I would have been if it had been Mama in the same situation, and I just... Oh, to hell with it. I don't see why I have to explain myself to you. We were both there, you saw exactly what happened. I don't know why you're so jealous." A wave of anger was rising in Jonty, and there wasn't likely to be an ebb in this tide any time soon.

"Because you obviously like him and he likes you." Orlando studied his shoes.

"Then you should be jealous of Mrs. Tattersall, or Mr. Tattersall. Half the English fellows and who knows who else, I like them all. Stop being an idiot."

"You don't put your arm around the English fellows. You don't get sent for to talk Mr. Tattersall out of suicide." Orlando tired of addressing his shoes and spoke to Jonty's shirt buttons.

"You were the one he tried to kiss, not me. He's never shown the slightest inclination to do anything with me."

"I suppose you regret that."

Jonty had taken enough. He swung out an arm and clonked his friend on the chest, a hefty blow such as he'd employed on a lock forward or two in his time, when the referee was looking elsewhere. Orlando, winded, fell back onto the settee. "I've never hit you before, but I'll damn well do it again if this nonsense doesn't stop. I have no desire to do anything with Matthew Ainslie. I've not even looked at another man since I met you, even from that first night when you were so stuffy. Why you have the temerity to accuse me of such things is beyond me."

"Afraid I'll lose you." Orlando had begun to regain his breath. "That would be the end of my world. I'd not forget to load the pistol then."

Jonty looked at him, rolling his eyes. "Overdramatising again, are we? Blackmail is a horrible thing—I'll not be kept at your side by it. You can't play the leave-me-and-I'll-kill-myself card because I'll ignore it. I have no intention of leaving you as things stand, I love you far too much, but my patience isn't infinite. There's only so much self-pity I can put up with. Or stupidity."

Orlando swallowed hard. He could guess what was coming

next—it had been brewing for months. "I'm sorry."

"Sometimes sorry isn't good enough. I think I'm getting to understand you and then I realise I have no bloody idea what goes on in your brain." Jonty pointed to his bedroom. "Why won't you...in there... Why won't you do it properly? Well, the answer's not in your bloody shoes so don't look at them for it."

"I'm frightened, is that enough for you? I'm scared you'll hurt me or I'll hurt you and we'll end up hating each other." Painful pinpricks of fear broke out on Orlando's brow. "My mother loathed it. That's why there's just me and not a houseful like your family has."

Jonty didn't look as if he believed it. "How would you know? I thought the Coppersmiths never stooped so low as to discuss these things?"

"We didn't." Clenching of sweaty hands into fists. "I overheard them talking once, my mother and father. I didn't understand at the time. I do now."

Somewhere in the distance a child was laughing, a reminder of the brood who filled the Stewart house on high days and holidays. "Is this true?" Jonty's voice was shaky.

"Not a word of a lie." Orlando addressed his shoes.

"I'm so sorry."

"I don't want you being sorry for me."

"It's not just that. I'm sorry for us." The shaky voice was barely more than a whisper, now. "I love you, Orlando, but I'm not sure how we proceed from here."

There was no appropriate answer.

Jonty slipped off to the bathroom, saying with a wan smile, "I'm going to have a soak and use up all the hot water so *you* can't have one. That'll serve you right for being a cantankerous old puss."

And leaving Orlando to wonder how things could have gone

so horribly wrong so quickly.

📖

Before dinner they took drinks in the bar as usual, a constrained politeness between them, although they were soon intrigued at the sight of Mrs. Tattersall unravelling a fluffy white half-finished item.

She smiled at them wistfully. "Daft, isn't it? I can't get this completed now, as I've only one needle. Think I lost the other one that first night you came. I've searched high and low but to no avail. Mr. T reckons I was so taken with you two that I stuffed it down the side of one of the chairs in a mad moment. He's probably right."

Walking on eggshells carried on through to the end of dinner, despite Mr. Tattersall dropping his glasses in his consommé, sending little savoury droplets in all directions and making everyone laugh. They made up a bridge four, Orlando rather pleased that Matthew had decided to play chess with Mr. Newlywed while Mrs. Newlywed looked on admiringly, annoying everyone with her constant stream of chat, all of it centred on her beloved Anthony. Bridge was concluded early, Mrs. Tattersall feeling rather tired, but the two young men were less keen than usual to escape to the refuge of their suite.

Eventually they retired, Jonty having perhaps one port too many inside him. "Orlando," he purred, full of food and drink and so slightly happier with life, "do you really feel like a, what was the delightful expression you used yesterday, a *kept man*?"

"Not in college, Jonty. But sometimes when we're out, off to the theatre or here on holidays, it always seems to be you footing the bill."

"It's purely a matter of logic. You of all people must appreciate that. I have plenty of money and nothing to spend it on except my own pleasure, of which you are the summit of all my joys."

"I'm not a pauper, you realise that." Orlando produced one of his sternest frowns to support his assertion.

"I do realise. You'll note that I'm wearing one of the shirts you bought me at the end of last term to mark the end of the academic year. Romantic as always." Jonty couldn't stop a stream of tipsy giggles issuing forth.

"I've been thinking."

"Really? Not something you indulge in that often. Ow. Don't whack me."

"Is there no way in which we could share the expenses equally?"

"Not without ending up in an argument about the overall costs or resenting one another for having different amounts of ready cash. Look, Orlando, it's like a scalene triangle," Jonty had thought of what he no doubt felt was a clever allusion. "The angles are all different, aren't they? Every triangle doesn't have to be equilateral or even isosceles. I bet the little fifteen-degree angle doesn't get cross with the filthy great ninety-five-degree one because it's bigger."

Orlando began to laugh. He didn't stop until he was having trouble breathing and Jonty had slapped him very hard on the back, making the giggling stop with an enormous hiccup. "I've never heard such nonsense in all my life. Scalene triangles—I bet you can't even spell the word, let alone know what it means. If that's the best logical reasoning you can produce, then there's no point arguing with you. Pay what you like, spend what you like, I'll never complain again."

It was the wrong choice of words, the truce broken again. Chablis and port might have mellowed Jonty for a while, but they'd lowered the threshold of belligerence. "I wish that was so in bed. We can't go on like this forever."

"Your Lavinia does with her Ralph, or so you keep telling me." The Chablis had made Orlando as bold as it had made his lover truculent. "They probably don't even have what we do. And yet they soldier on."

"But I don't want to soldier on. I'm not asking for every moment of the day to be wonderful—that would be deathly boring for a start—but I don't want this to be something we have to bear, being all noble in the name of love."

"So what do we do?"

"No bloody idea, Orlando. I wish I could wave some magic wand and change what goes on in here," Jonty gently ruffled his lover's hair. "But if you're still so very frightened after all these months I'm not sure I have the answer."

Chapter Ten

"This really is very kind of you to ask me for a walk, Mr. Ainslie. I don't want you thinking that I go walking with just any gentleman from the Beaulieu." The maid from the hotel was clearly enjoying the luxury of walking down to the harbour in the sunshine with one of the guests, and had donned a neat little green summer frock in honour of the occasion.

Matthew inclined his head with a kind smile. Monday afternoon had seemed a long time coming once the idea of a little detective work had been mooted. He'd eagerly anticipated it, not least because it gave him something to do, a bit of a purpose to his sad, empty days. "No, I understand that entirely, Miss...?"

"Brabazon." The maid's bright blue eyes sparkled. She was quite a pretty thing, if you were that way inclined.

"Ah, that's not a local name, is it?"

"No, it ain't. Sorry, isn't. My father came over here as the chef a good five years ago. Mother died when I was a little girl."

Matthew produced a sympathetic nod.

"So I came with him. I like it, very much. Hard work but nothing to complain about, and the food is lovely." Miss Brabazon looked like the sort of girl who would appreciate her food.

"Well, Miss Brabazon, I asked you to come for a walk so

that I could express my gratitude to you for being so kind over the last week since my father died. You've looked after my room very nicely—I appreciate the way you've kept his things so tidy, despite the best efforts of the police to disarrange them."

"That's very kind of you, sir. Just my job, really."

"You have such a lot of rooms to keep clean, it must be a chore. I bet that Miss Sheringham causes you a lot of work."

The maid gave a toss of her auburn curls, ringlets which couldn't have been that particular colour before the odd chemical had got to work. "Oh, *madam*. Her friend's as bad. I don't do *her* room, Martha does, and you should hear what she has to say about Miss Forbes." The maid stopped, no doubt afraid she'd said far too much. Matthew tried to put on his most encouraging look. "I shouldn't say so, but young ladies are often the most trouble."

"I would think *that* lady in particular causes you a problem or two, they're quite a presumptuous family, in my experience. Indeed, I find them rather unfriendly towards me. I have no idea why." Matthew wasn't sure he could wear a convincingly innocent face, nevertheless he gave it his best shot.

"I did hear say that his company is a rival to yours, perhaps that's it. Jealousy about how well your business is doing."

"You're probably right. It's not as if they have anything else against me, is it?"

Alice coloured slightly, suddenly greatly interested in the sea. "Don't think so, Mr. Ainslie." The answer was so obviously a lie that she might as well have said, "I've heard the story, I know about the letters." She changed the subject. "Lovely day today, it's nice to have a break."

"I hope that you get a well-deserved rest as often as you can. I would hazard that some of the young gentlemen at the hotel make plenty of offers of entertainment."

"Mr. Ainslie! I'm a nice girl. What would my Alec say if he heard you speak so?"

"I meant no impropriety, my dear, only that you must receive many an unwelcome offer. I knew you were too sensible to fall for any saucy young buck's chat."

"I should think so too. But I don't want to be working here all my life. Alec would love to set up a little pub on his own. I could cook and he'd run the bar. You'll have seen him behind the bar here, Mr. Ainslie, very good he is with the clientele."

"Are you sure he doesn't mind you taking a little stroll with me?"

"Oh, not at all. 'You go along with him,' he said. 'He seems a nice man.'"

Matthew observed her closely out of the corner of his eye, however this time what she said seemed to be the truth. "Realistically, what are your chances of finding a little place to run?"

"Good enough if we had the money, sir, but that's the rub, as my dad says. Difficult enough to put anything by these days. Alec's working all the hours he can here and he's desperate to pick up any other bits of casual employment so he can put by a bit extra." She sighed.

"Does he do any extra work in the hotel or just tend the bar?"

"Just that, officially. The Beaulieu's well staffed, doesn't need any extra hands at present. Although I think he might help the boots and the laundry on the quiet for a share of the tips with no questions asked."

"I wonder if he may have done something for my father? I would hate to have him go without a gratuity if he deserved one."

"No." It was just a fraction too long a pause. "I don't think he helped your poor papa, sir. I think he's done a bit of valeting

154

for the Sheringhams, their own man having been struck down with food poisoning two weeks back. Food poisoning, I ask you, sir. He shouldn't have been eating winkles from a stall like a barrow boy, should he?"

"Indeed not." Matthew's thoughts had turned to food not for the stomach but for thought. "Your Alec sounds a very able chap—he's a lucky man to have such a nice girl as you. I hope that you'll be very happy together."

The maid's face crumpled in dismay just a little. Matthew understood the situation in that one small look. No doubt she was fond of her young man, but many girls had a pragmatic streak. He was a very eligible quantity, a little flirtation with him might have led to some nice rewards, except he'd brought the shutters down very firmly on that possibility. Alice would have to keep with her Alec and his dreams, at least for the time being. She managed a smile, her training in never showing her true feelings to her betters standing her in good stead. "That's most kind of you, sir. I just hope that Alec can make as much of himself as you've done."

They walked back to the hotel surrounded by an air of disappointment on the lady's part and thoughtfulness on the man's. Matthew desperately wanted to discuss this conversation with his two new friends, but they'd gone off in the morning to look at some ancient monuments on the far side of the island then were stopping off en route home to see a concert in the park at St. Helier. He'd have to bide his time, content with an afternoon's cribbage with Mr. Tattersall.

The sound of the band tuning up drifted softly over the air, exciting Jonty's senses to an alarming degree if the look in his eyes was anything to go by. "Just like the orchestra starting up before a show, Orlando. Always sets all my nerves a-tingle and sends shivers up my spine." He was happier today, determined to enjoy himself, as he always was when adversity struck. They'd got through troubles before—Orlando had to believe they'd get through this latest crisis.

They walked over the grass to where the crowd was already beginning to settle for the concert. The little bandstand shone delightfully, looking like a toy in a shop window at Christmas, just a little too perfect to be used for anything except admiring. However, a small brass band had crammed themselves into it and were busy making arrangements to play.

They obtained two deckchairs, gaudy striped contraptions which resembled the worst kind of pyjamas. For once, Jonty was bested, Orlando being immediately able to work out how to erect the awkward thing then watching with delight as his friend went from crisis to crisis in his vain attempt to get his chair to fit together properly.

"Shall I?"

"You'd better, or I'll take a hammer to the thing."

A quick flip, and the seat was in its rightful position. "See? Easy."

Jonty muttered something that might just have ended in "-ugger", but wasn't "rugger", then sat down. He soon cheered up when the band struck up a Strauss waltz, drumming the beat on his thighs with strong fingers. The end of the piece was met with loud applause from the audience, the quality of the music being much appreciated. The joie de vivre of the players infected everyone, not a hard feat as the day was fine and holiday spirit abounded.

The next item was a rather naughty medley of music hall tunes, the words of which were happily sung among the crowd, followed by a selection of light orchestral pieces. During one of these, Orlando nudged his friend in the side and pointed to an elderly couple in front of them who, having struggled to put up their one deck chair, were now attempting to share it. "I think we should give them one of ours, Jonty."

"Of course, I'll take mine over." He looked a bit sheepish and stared at the grass. "If you'll just fold it, of course."

Orlando's bosom swelled with pride and he mentally listed this as being another area in which he had supremacy over the light of his life. Bridge, racing tips, croquet, catching shrimps, putting up deckchairs, making his lover moan—the list was becoming nicely lengthened. He deftly returned the chair to its flat state, waved aside all offers of help, took it over to the couple, then just as deftly erected it again, bowing politely. Jonty was grinning with pleasure, standing up to stretch himself while the band searched out their music for the next tune.

Orlando indicated his own chair. "Take mine, I can sit on the grass."

"You will not. We'll take turn and turn about, one piece of music each. We're not in the Senior Common Room now with rules about keeping to particular seats. I've already been accused, very early on in our friendship, of stealing your special chair. I shan't risk it again."

They'd set the deckchairs up at the very back of the crowd, where they were likely to be unobserved as all the eyes and ears were turned forwards to the bandstand. The height of the backs of the chairs made it very difficult to see over them anyway, except if you took advantage of the slight rise at the side of the arena.

Jonty gently lowered his posterior to the grass, a process which gave him a strange view of a world peopled by rear ends encompassed by sagging striped canvas. He gradually manoeuvred himself until he was by Orlando's knees, then surreptitiously lifted his arm, resting it on one of them. The music carried on, a variation on the "1812 Overture" being attempted as a first half finale, and Orlando was so wrapped up in the piece he didn't notice what was happening. Jonty grew bolder, moving his head across until it rested on his own arm, the one which lay upon his lover's knee. It was about the closest he'd come to Orlando in broad daylight, in public—the thrill was delicious. He was wondering whether there was any way that he could get his nose to make contact with the man's flesh when his head got thrown violently in the air by the jerk of a bony kneecap.

"What do you think you're playing at, you little pest?" Orlando hissed like some agitated serpent.

"Seeing how far I could go without you noticing, of course," Jonty whispered his reply. "Got quite a way really, my main objective being to get my nose in contact with a part of your exposed flesh." He laughed. "Quite a good game this, I must try it again."

"Well you won't do it here. I'm wise to you now, troublemaker." Orlando almost giggled, something which happened very rarely in public.

They sat back as the concert re-started with some Vivaldi. Orlando listened with initial pleasure tempered by increasing distress, the swell and grandeur of the music making him think of the passion he and Jonty had shared so often in the past. The nagging voice in his brain, the one he'd been trying to ignore these last few days, suggested it would remain in the past and all he'd be left with were memories. Jonty wanted change; he wanted things to stay the same. Impasse.

The voice—the haunting, eminently believable voice—was making him uncomfortable, so he turned his mind to the comforting topic of murder. Matthew was out doing the questioning, the part of the procedure which Orlando liked the least, although he still wasn't sure he trusted the man to tell them the truth about what he'd found.

Orlando desperately wanted to unravel the mystery before the police did, not through any malice for Wilson or le Tissier but from the sheer thrill of the chase and the delights of an intellectual puzzle solved. And because it would take his mind off what happened the night before.

Orlando's brain kept ticking over, exploring avenues. He could clearly formulate a theory about one of the staff finding the accusatory letters in Sheringham's drawer, using the information, flawed as it was, to start a little scheme of his or her own. All that was missing was the evidence that such a thing had happened. He inwardly laughed at how he'd have ripped apart any thesis from his students that didn't follow the strict Coppersmith *evidence first, theory second* rule. They should hoist him on his own petard here, and a pretty explosion it would make. Frustratingly, the theory, neat as it was, still didn't bring them any closer to finding the murderer.

If Ainslie senior had found out about the letters then confronted the blackmailer, possibly they might have panicked and killed him, but how would any blackmailer have got around the back of his victim without raising the man's suspicions? Had there been two people working in concert? A collaborator of the letter writer, apparently an innocent party to Ainslie, might be the answer. Someone who could have come in on another pretext—the maid to re-hang a curtain, perhaps—that person could have quite easily dealt the blow.

So could his son. Matthew Ainslie still seemed the most logical suspect, the neatest solution to the case. He could have returned to his room earlier than he'd said, got into another row with his father, killed him and then constructed some sort of dramatic 'finding of the body'. And if he'd used his tiepin, the police would likely never find it—it would have been thrown into the harbour days ago.

The concert came to its loud and dramatic end, people struggled to put down deckchairs while Orlando smugly watched them, then folk walked off to coaches or train stations humming the most popular melodies. Time was drawing on, so he and Jonty wandered down to the quay to take a cab back to the Beaulieu.

They had barely time to change for dinner before they were due to meet Matthew in a quiet corner of the bar, summoned by an intriguing note they found pushed under the door on their return.

📖

Matthew's eyes were all aglow with his information. "Nothing you could rely on in court," he averred. "Just some juicy little titbits that bear consideration if you'll let me share the fruit of my thinking." He'd chosen a table where they were unlikely to be overheard. "If Alice had got an inkling about those letters, perhaps she'd mentioned them to her Alec." He tipped his head towards the barman, who was busy serving the newlyweds, a couple who were starting to look just a little tired as the fortnight progressed. "He wants to increase his funds, has his sights set higher than keeping someone else's bar, and he gets to visit the guests' rooms. What if he found the papers in Sheringham's rooms then just repeated the allegations verbatim? He could have had his letters under my door soon enough, and the method of reply seems more suited to a local rather than a visitor."

Orlando studied his glass for a while. "I never even saw those letters—Jonty won't share their contents with me. He probably thinks I'm not mature enough. Would you tell me what the accusations were and how they were substantiated?"

Jonty turned to Orlando, incredulous at his effrontery. He was demonstrating yet again how much he'd got to grips with life outside St. Bride's. The old Orlando would never have been so bold, although there had always been a masterly streak lying dormant within him. Jonty had seen that the night of the first murder at Bride's, when the man had taken control of events—

since then it had only shown itself on odd occasions, like at the Derby.

If only he'd be so courageous in bed.

Jonty began to colour at the remembrance of the previous evening and hastily spoke. "Would you be happy to tell us, Matthew? I know what was said in those vile things, although I've no idea, apart from your assertions of what was untrue, how much could be proven."

Matthew stared at his hands, as he had stared at Orlando's the night before his father was killed. "The letter writer stated he, or she, knew that I lay with men and pointed out that this wasn't just illegal but, in his view, immoral. While I disagree with the last point, the rest is true. There were allegations made that I had paid for boys to..." He coloured slightly. "To provide me with services, at certain hotels. That is *not* true, I've never had to pay to make anyone take my favours. I find the idea of that abhorrent, anyway, as no doubt you both do. There also was a suggestion that I kept a young man in accommodation at my cost, like men keep their mistresses. This is also not in any way accurate, though I've made presents to one or two of my friends in the past. Tokens of my esteem."

Jonty smiled as he saw Orlando trying not to look down at his tiepin, which might well qualify in the same category as Matthew's *tokens*. Tiepins. The place was awash with the things.

"If these allegations are untrue," Orlando said, "there would be nothing with which to substantiate them, so what would you have to fear?"

"Oh, I know full well that nothing could be made to hold up in court on these counts, unless someone were prepared to bribe a witness. Why on earth should anyone seek to see themselves out of pocket on that score? There might be some leeway in misinterpreting the gifts I gave my friends, but I think not. The simple truth is that these men were more than friends

161

to me, and one of them I parted with on less-than-happy terms. If he's seen fit to supply Sheringham's agent with information..."

"I think I see a possible chain of events here." Orlando sat forward, his eyes keen. "I understand Sheringham's been pally for years with Forbes, who's your rival in business. Neither of them seemed to bear your father any love. Perhaps they've been waiting for an opportunity of harming your reputation, both personal and commercial. Let's say Sheringham somehow stumbles across your friend, the embittered one, they fall to talking about the printing business in general, your name comes up and certain accusations are made in spite. They say hell hath no fury like a woman scorned—I dare say men can hold their own on that point too. Sheringham says he needs things in writing, with details of some specific incidents, as soon as possible, however this has all happened too close to his holiday, so the information has to be sent here."

Jonty snorted. "Aren't you breaking your own rules again about basing theories on evidence? You'd flay your students for doing the same."

"Probably, but I don't care. This freedom from the university practice of academic rigour and rectitude is exhilarating."

"Alright, Sheringham gets the letter with the details he requires. What then?" Jonty was almost bouncing with eagerness to see what stunning conclusions his friend had reached.

"Then he takes his chance. By one of life's strange coincidences, the Ainslie family is staying here, so he strikes while the iron is hot, seeing this as a way to increase his funds and do his friend Forbes some good in the process, and sends the blackmailing note, unaware that Matthew's friend has told him a pack of lies."

"So far it makes some sense, despite the fact that it seems

to be the complete opposite of what you said yesterday. But I guess that mathematicians are likely to be a bit changeable. *La don e mobile,* what?" Jonty giggled, as did Matthew, who appreciated the exceedingly bad operatic pun.

Orlando simply made a rude face at his friend. "I'm ignoring those comments. I'm merely re-exploring all the possibilities now that I have more information, some of which I didn't have previously."

Matthew looked as though he was fighting hard to hide a grin, his blue eyes burning with intense concentration. "I have less and less inclination to accept that theory about Sheringham. The man isn't short of money—and if he was helping his friend, the motive would surely be to disgrace us, not to fleece us. Forbes would probably be better off financially with a rival out of the way, rather than risking being in court himself involved with extortion. I accept that the information may well have come as you suggest, but I think someone else used it. I wouldn't be surprised if that someone was in the room now." A little inclination of the head toward the bar. "What do you think, Jonty?"

Jonty started. "Oh, I'm sorry, I was woolgathering again. I think Orlando is possibly right about the source of those accusations. If you've been discreet, then it's unlikely you've left an incriminating trail, so they'll have come from someone close. There's much to be said, Matthew, for your choice of suspect for blackmail. Although murder is quite another thing."

Orlando rolled his eyes, implying that Jonty was only a poor student of the Bard, not equipped with a mathematician's academic rigidity.

"You can sneer if you want to, Orlando, but I feel you're both making this thing too complex. We potentially have someone collecting information, or making it up more like, another man to whom this gen is given, then another person who comes along, notes or copies the stuff and uses it for blackmail. Does he or she commit the murder? No, it's his, or her, accomplice who does the deed."

"Accomplice?"

"Yes, Matthew. Orlando feels that your father was far too sensible to let a blackmailer walk around behind him, so he's introduced some other person, one your father would have trusted, who got behind his defences. Stuff and nonsense." Jonty waited for Orlando to justify his theory, but none came. "I believe there was great passion at work in your father's murder, and significant physical strength too. I'm not sure that, say, Alice would either feel moved enough to commit the deed or have the power to do it. It can't be easy to..." He stopped, Realising he had overstepped the bounds of decency. "Alec might well have qualified on both counts, if he were desperate enough."

Matthew looked puzzled at this new development to an already complex theory.

"Suddenly an expert on Ockham's Razor, are we, Jonty?" Orlando was still undoubtedly miffed about the *la donna e mobile* joke.

"Never pretended to be, it's just common sense not to create some over-elaborate scenario. And a bit of gut feeling, talking of which, is that waiter ever coming with the menu? Because I feel fair clemmed again."

"You're always fair clemmed, you must have worms," Orlando countered, "or hollow legs."

The gathering dissolved into laughter, anticipation of dinner being much more welcome than considering the labyrinth this case was becoming.

Chapter Eleven

Tuesday brought another scorching hot day in prospect. From the moment they'd rather daringly taken their early morning teas out onto the balcony, Jonty and Orlando had begun to plan their swim. They knew they would be safe from peeping Toms, or peeping Mavises, as the "Misses" were going into St. Helier to look for new outfits with which to astound their male admirers.

Jonty's view on hearing this was that there couldn't be enough material on the whole of Jersey to make a dress for Miss Forbes, who wasn't a small girl. He also speculated that Miss Sheringham's family would be better off waiting for the races and seeing if there was a supplier of horse blankets present. It was really very rude of him, hardly displaying his usual magnanimity, excusable only because he'd taken extreme umbrage with these young hussies over their spying on him. He had no doubt it was *deliberate* spying, that they'd been on his—and Orlando's—trail. As Ainslie senior had probably followed his son.

This time, when they arrived at *their* bay, the only inhabitants to be observed on the cliffs were some sand martins darting about looking for insects, so the men were free to strip down to their costumes on the beach then run down to the sea. They stopped just short of the waves, astounded at what they found on the sand there. Starfish—red golden, creamy white, large as plates, small as a penny—dozens of them, strewn along the strand.

"Where have they come from?"

"Wind got up last night. I heard it even if you were dead to the world. Combination of that alongside a strong sea drove them in and cast them up on the shore, I guess. It seems so sad."

Orlando gingerly picked one up, observing the slow movement of its limbs, then gently put it back into the surf, only to see it be stranded again. "Is there nothing we can do?"

"Cast them back, I suppose, as far as we can throw them and away from the rocks." Several of the things were already missing limbs where they'd been thumped against the stones with all the force the waves could muster, as if the sea itself was intent on destroying them. The men began to pick the creatures up, flinging them out to the place where the beach fell away steeply.

"Do you think that we can save them?"

"I don't know, Orlando. Truly"

"But we should try?"

"Oh, yes. If we can make a difference to just one, then it's been worthwhile." When all the handsome little beasts had been sent flying, the men stopped to watch the crashing surf, wondering how many of the things that they'd rescued were just being smashed up again. Jonty waited for what he thought would be an inevitable remark from his friend about how *he* felt like one of those starfish and how Jonty had rescued him, but the comment didn't come. He felt relieved, as sometimes Orlando was just too mawkish for comfort, yet from the corner of his eye he could see a sentimental look on his face, a look which needed to be got rid of quickly.

"Race you to the rock pools, slowcoach. Last one there buys lunch all the rest of the week." Jonty hared off like billy-oh, leaving Orlando in his wake, a state of affairs that didn't last for long. "One day you will be kind enough to let me win for once." Jonty was bent over, hands on knees, huffing and puffing like a great whale.

"The kindness wouldn't be to your ultimate good. You're quite insufferable enough already about your many accomplishments. You must accept that I'm the faster runner. Always will be." Orlando grinned.

Jonty began plotting an elaborate revenge. Involving mild-to-moderate bodily pain. And a lobster.

"I'll get even with you, Orlando. I'll tell Mavis that you have such a passion for her, you'd like to meet her by the fountain tonight."

"You wouldn't dare, not in a million years."

"Wouldn't I just? No, I suppose I wouldn't, you're right. Perhaps I can meet you by the fountain instead. I seem to remember that was the start of a very memorable evening. As I recall you…"

"Sh! You mustn't speak of such things in public."

"Public? How does two oystercatchers, a turnstone and some starfish—the bloody things are coming in again, Orlando—constitute public?"

"It just does."

"I suppose those starfish are going to write down every word we speak—they'd be good at that given the number of arms they have—then give it to Inspector Wilson, who would be supremely indifferent to it, I suspect. That would teach the little buggers, and they'd have to go home to the bottom of the sea shame-faced. Only they don't seem to have faces, so it would be red-bodied."

"You talk such twaddle at times. If anyone had told me a year ago I'd be intoxicated listening to someone going on about what part of a starfish turned red when they were embarrassed,

I'd have thought they'd gone totally mad. But it's not madness, is it? It's love." He took Jonty into his arms, out by the rocks, in full view of the sea and the cliff tops, then kissed him. "Whatever happens, don't you ever forget."

The police were just about twenty-four hours behind the combined intellects of Matthew, Orlando and Jonty in the matter of the hotel staff. Or so it appeared to Matthew, when he was summoned back to the little room where interviews took place. It seemed they'd questioned Alice, receiving much the same information as he had, although he suspected it wasn't given as freely or with such goodwill. She'd not been able to hide the fact that she'd overheard Gwenny Sheringham being told about the letters by her father, or that she'd then related the story to Alec Banks.

"We wondered whether Banks could have looked for the letters when he was doing his valeting and whether he would have been inclined to use them to draft his own missives." If Inspector Wilson knew he was behindhand on the trail, he didn't show it.

"What did he have to say for himself?" Matthew was aware that, as a suspect, he should be answering the questions not posing them, but his amateur sleuthing had made him bold.

"Very little, like he'd put up shutters of steel. There was the usual nonsense of insisting he'd been told nothing by Alice, who, if looks are anything to go by, is in for a tongue-lashing once he gets hold of her. *Letters?* He didn't know the first thing about them, either." Le Tissier sniffed. "He says all he did was valeting for Mr. Sheringham and cleaning the shoes for all the family."

"He said we could check all the blades kept behind the bar

if we want, but he swore he'd never taken or used them for any purpose other than what they were designed for. Doesn't have his own one, either." Wilson's face showed how little he believed any of it.

"And so?" Denials, lies. Were they any nearer the truth of things?

"We had to allow him to return to his job, on the understanding that, like several other people here, he's not to leave the island. We need to find some other witness who can contribute information on what Banks has been up to. There's one thing you can help us with." Wilson drew some envelopes from his inside pocket. "Perhaps you might be able to help us by putting a name to the author?"

Matthew didn't blanch when he saw the writing; he'd steeled himself to see something familiar so wasn't overly surprised. Of course he could name the person who'd shopped him to Sheringham. Nonetheless, his heart was torn to observe such spite in the familiar handwriting, script which before had spoken only of tenderness. Elegant whorls that had described endearments and passion now told of lies and anger. The author was Alistair Stafford, a man Matthew once thought he could have loved.

He sighed, folded the papers, returned them. "I'm sorry, gentlemen. I can't tell who has written these."

"And you still can't tell us what became of your tiepin?"

"I have no idea. Perhaps Banks took it—a little payment in advance?" The heat under Matthew's collar increased.

Le Tissier shook his greying head. "This problem's proving as slippery as an eel and just as liable to twist itself into knots when it thinks itself caught. Give me a nice straightforward case where men are stabbed to death by their wives for kissing the parlour maid or ancient aunts get poisoned for the profit of their beneficiaries."

"Ah, there's the rub." Wilson looked as if he too would rather be investigating a pub brawl. "There's nothing so simple here. Whoever killed your father, Mr. Ainslie, has been very clever, or very lucky, or both." The look he gave Matthew suggested Wilson thought he possessed both those qualities.

📖

The soft double bed in the Beaulieu's best suite hadn't seen anyone *do their duty* for a while, except in the detection sense. Orlando had made a list for them to go through, item by item.

Possible weapons—the hotel was bristling with them, from Greenwood's tiepin to the lethal-looking thing that Mrs. Newlywed kept her hat on with. According to Wilson, many of these nasty little items had been examined and all had proved relatively spotless.

"Perhaps that's suspicious in itself, Jonty?"

"I doubt it. People like to keep things clean, especially when they have servants to do the cleaning for them." Jonty wrinkled his nose thoughtfully. "What have you got listed under opportunity?"

Orlando snorted like a grumpy horse. "That's worse. I feel at times that the whole island could have come in and caused mayhem in that room. The police say all their attempts at logical elimination have proved futile. You'll be pleased about that, with your hatred of alibis." He turned a page. "Then there are possible motives. Those are crawling out of the dark like woodlice when you turn a garden pot."

"Well, I think you can discount infidelity, not just because of what Matthew said about his father. Lady Hardley should be scratched from your race card."

"Even with the fact that Mr. Greenwood knows Lord Hardley from the London club where he once worked? Or Mr.

Newlywed being a distant relation of his lordship?"

"Red herrings, both of 'em. I trust my mother implicitly in this. You'd be better off considering sharp practice at the tables—several people have mentioned things Ainslie allegedly did, including accusing other people of cheating. What if one of the guests here had been a victim of the man's skulduggery? That evening before he died—what if he'd been at it again and someone took umbrage?"

"Come to that, you can't discount business rivalry. I'd love to know if there's a concerted attempt to embarrass Ainslie's publishing house. Perhaps it's just fierce rivalry, but there's been more than one hint that things weren't at all rosy in the garden when Charles Ainslie was in charge of the business." Orlando tapped his notes in frustration. "It's all hints or gossip, nothing concrete to get our teeth into."

"That blackmail's concrete enough. I can't decide whether it's just some opportunist trying to make some easy money, or if there are deeper motives at work." Jonty's fingers traced the word *murder,* which stood out among his friend's notes. "There's passion here, Orlando. Real passion, enough to take a man's life in cold blood. Someone hated Ainslie enough to take his life. If you want a nice conundrum to go to sleep with, think long and hard about whom we've come across who's given us a hint of something like zeal for revenge."

"His son wasn't enamoured of him, was he? I can vouch for Matthew Ainslie's passion."

"You won't let it drop, will you?" Jonty shook his head. "And I have an awful feeling the police agree with you. All this blackmail business points towards Matthew, not away from him. What a bloody mess."

They lay in silence for a while. "Sleeping here tonight?" Orlando fingered his lover's pyjama jacket.

"Yes. I think I've got so used to it now, it'll be an awful

shock going back to college. Just sleeping, though." Jonty stroked his Orlando's face. "Until we get this mess—these messes—sorted out."

📖

First thing Wednesday morning they looked for Matthew; a visit to St. Brelade's bay was on the cards and Orlando had proposed they invite him along. Jonty had even suggested keeping Matthew's acquaintance when they returned home. The man would enjoy coming up to High Table as their guest and heaven knows he would need good friends to support him in the future.

Matthew, however, wasn't to be found. It was said he'd left early for the station—an appointment in St. Helier, Mrs. Tattersall believed—leaving no messages.

"Well, it's just us then. Shame, though. I think Matthew would have appreciated the church and its graveyard. Bet he's as keen on the places as I am."

Orlando frowned. He'd hoped that church visiting was done with for this holiday, but Jonty obviously had other ideas. He would need to hatch a little plan or two to get round it.

"Penny for your thoughts, Orlando? You seem unusually pensive today, even by your standards."

Orlando started, caught out in his fantasies about faking a bad leg or a rash or anything else that would prevent the torture of another set of pews. "Oh, I was just wondering what business could have taken Matthew into town at such an early hour." It was the other direction his thoughts were taking. Matthew Ainslie "doing a runner".

"Probably an entirely innocent motive, I'd say. Waiting for something or someone arriving on the early boat. Seeing a doctor. I don't know, and I'm not going to spoil the day speculating." He turned his attention to a particularly scrumptious sausage. "I must find out which butcher they use here, these are possibly the finest bangers I've ever tasted. We could have them sent to Bride's, acquire a little stove, then I could cook them for you for Sunday breakfast, after our usual visit to the Bishop's Cope."

Orlando blushed, hurriedly raising his teacup to his lips to try to hide his burning cheeks. Visits to the Bishop's Cope usually ended up with port in his rooms then a night in his bed. He hissed for his friend to be quiet.

Jonty just laughed. He was in a wonderful mood for some reason known only to himself, and nothing that Orlando could do would spoil it.

They finished their meal in relative peace, returning to their room to read the previous day's newspaper before they left for their excursion. Orlando found a scandalous tale about his old professor at Oxford which he could hardly bear to read, involving as it did not one but *two* kept women. They pored over every little story, feeling very out of touch with the real world in this almost fairytale land of sea and sand and long hot days. Once replete with news, they priddied themselves to a peak of beauty then set off to stun the world.

📖

"Not another churchyard, please, I beg of you. I've been in every church on this island, I've seen the grave of every man, woman, child and goat who has died these last thousand years." Orlando sat on a little wall by the side of the road, refusing to budge. He'd been unable to devise any more effective a strategy than non-cooperation, but he hoped it would be successful. Perhaps Jonty would take a sympathetic view, then they could go and play lawn bowls somewhere. Or annoy squirrels. Anything except visiting churches.

"This is one of the loveliest places of worship on the island. St. Brelade's, you know, has a great reputation. There's a little fisherman's chapel and—"

"You've said that every church we've been to is one of the loveliest. None of them have been in any way mediocre by your reckoning. Not before or during or afterwards."

"But we've seen such stained glass, such brasses." Jonty's eyes lit up with rapture.

Orlando remembered all of the brasses—he'd been made to translate most of them, his Latin being sounder than Jonty's. If he saw another parsimonious inscription to another saintly being snatched in their prime he would be adding his friend to the list. He'd hide the body in the sand dunes and run away to sea before he was caught.

"Just this one, Orlando. Just this one then there'll be no more until advent. Just chapel on Sundays. And Wednesdays for evensong. Not forgetting St George's when we stay with the family."

Orlando capitulated, as he always did when Jonty had set his heart on something, but the long walk down to the church was done in relative silence, the mathematician calculating how much sand it would take to bury a body and whether the rate at which it would be blown away would allow him to get to the other side of the world by steamship.

The church was beautiful, unbelievably so, with a glorious roof which made the whole thing feel snug and welcoming, instead of overpowering as so many places of worship were. As soon as they stepped through the door, the atmosphere affected them. They dutifully processed around the building, reading the inscriptions, but even Jonty's heart was no longer in it. This was a place to be enjoyed in a different way. They sat in the pews, simply breathing in the smells of polished wood, the odour of the single candle burning, the aroma of the abundant leather-bound bibles.

"I often think that places capture a sense of what people have done in them. People have prayed here and found a touch of the world beyond this one. Peace, they've found that too, the very stones of the building ring with it." Jonty's eyes were aglow. He knew that his lover was a heathen at heart. He went to church like any good boy would do, but he didn't truly believe, not like Jonty did. Yet he couldn't stop trying to introduce Orlando to the great secret he'd found. "Can't you feel anything here?"

Orlando looked even more serious than usual. "There *is* something Jonty, but I can't put a name to it. Mathematical vocabulary rather lets one down in these circumstances, you know—you're far better off with your soaring prose. It does feel peaceful here, and special. More than that I can't say." For the second time that holiday they sat holding hands in a house of God, until they were interrupted by the door opening and the arrival of the verger.

Their plans for the rest of the day had been to take lunch in some little hostelry en route to the Beaulieu, then get their bathers with a view to visiting *their* cove. The weather had other ideas, however, ensuring they reached the hotel, without umbrella or coat, extremely wet. They ended up lying on the settee, listening to the showers caressing the window panes, which was an enormously pleasurable experience when one was at last dry, warm and indoors.

"Do you recall your final exams, Orlando, or does your poor senile brain struggle to remember that long ago?"

There was no spoken reply, just the application of knuckles to Jonty's head in a painful movement which was called a "nutmeg" when he was at school. Jonty didn't mind—the manifestation of mild violence was just a sign that he'd wound his lover up slightly and there was nothing Jonty enjoyed more than teasing a cross Orlando.

"I have a very good recollection of them—indeed I can tell

175

you exactly what the questions were. First there was..."

After ten minutes of details about not just the papers, but Orlando's brilliant responses to them, Jonty regretted he'd ever asked. He held up his hand to bring things to a halt.

"Fascinating as I find this, Orlando, I have to give a lecture in exactly—" he consulted his watch, "—six weeks, so I need to move our conversation on. What I meant to ask was whether there were any funny stories you had to tell from those times. I can vividly remember the first paper I took. This lad at the desk in front of me—he was huge, muscles in his spit—turned the paper over and simply burst into tears. The invigilators had to find someone to take him back to his college. Poor thing, he'd never once twigged in nearly three years that he hadn't been offered a place there on account of his intellect but because he was one of the finest rowers in England. Still, they gave him his degree. I suppose they had to, considering how much money his father had given to his college."

Orlando snorted, implying that *his* university would never have done such a thing, which was a lie, of course. He must have felt the need to go one better than his friend. "Now that you mention it, Jonty, there was a very peculiar thing happened in my final examination. We were all sitting working when we were aware of someone walking through the room—I distinctly remember every head going up at the same time to watch the man. Not that he made a lot of noise, just seemed to exude a rather noticeably cold presence that we'd all detected." He paused to observe his friend's reactions.

"Go on, Orlando." Jonty was fascinated.

"He was dressed in old-fashioned clothes, Georgian, I think, and seemed oblivious to us all working there. He simply progressed up the aisle between the desks, then exited directly through the oak-panelled wall. The invigilators didn't bat an eyelid, merely told us, 'Gentlemen, please carry on with your examination.' Turned out this ghost appeared quite regularly."

"How extraordinary! Did they know who he was?"

"It appears he was a student who had literally scared himself to death. When he was a child, his nurse had told him that if his hand ever grew larger than his face, then he would be dead within the week. It had become an obsession—he used to hold his hand up to his face every day to check. One day when he did so, he found it had grown larger overnight and he simply dropped dead from fright. So the nurse was proved correct."

Jonty shook his head, whistling incredulously. Gradually he raised his own hand to his face; Orlando must have known all along that he would, so he bided his time. As soon as Jonty's palm was immediately in front of his nose, Orlando's arm flew up and slapped his friend's hand into his own face.

There was an *Ow!* An oath. A red, crumpled little nose. Jonty sore and sheepish, angry at having been caught out. Orlando, triumphant for once, avenged for the church visit. His smugness didn't last very long. Jonty suddenly leaned forwards, put one hand to his face, cupped it as if catching something then dug in his pocket with the other. Great gobbets of blood started to stream from his nose, dropping into his hand and filling the hanky which was quickly stuffed to his nostrils.

"What's wrong?"

"Nosebleed, you clown. Give me your handkerchief." The clean linen stuffed into Jonty's bloodied, outstretched hand was used to replace his own, which he then thrust, red and wet, into Orlando's grasp. "Just need to pinch in the right place..." He fiddled around until he'd found a particular spot on the bridge of his nose where applying pressure made the torrent stop.

"Has this happened before?" Orlando was white as a ghost, with a look of plain terror on his face.

"Often when I was younger, especially on the rugby pitch. Thought I'd grown out of it. Wrong again." Jonty shifted his fingers to get a better grip. "Could do with another clean cloth."

Orlando didn't need to be asked twice—he quickly produced not only another immaculate handkerchief, but a wet flannel, with which he gently cleaned his lover's free hand. "I'm so very sorry, I only meant to have a bit of a laugh, like you've gulled me many a time. If I'd known, I would never have..." He looked up into Jonty's face at just the wrong moment. A strange effect of the back pressure from the nose pinching had caused blood to leak into his tear ducts and start flowing out of them.

Orlando had a buzzing feeling creep across his head, and a sensation like a big ugly forward had taken his legs from under him. "I think I'm going to..." He fainted.

📖

Pressing his hanky even closer to his poor face, Jonty leapt from the sofa to set off in search of the Tattersalls, whose room was only a few doors from the young men's. Mrs. T opened the door, Aloysius being in the middle of his late afternoon nap, grasped instantly what Jonty's problem was, listened sympathetically to what had happened to his friend then immediately offered to come along and help.

"Don't you go trying to pick him up, he's fine where he is," she said. "Just make sure he's on his side so he can breathe easily." He was; he could. "Now sit down with me and hold that nose of yours. Have you been pinching it a long time?"

"Hours it feels like, but I guess it's only been minutes."

"Well, hold it a minute more, then take the hanky away so I can get a look at it."

Gingerly, Jonty took his hand off his face, although he held it cupped below his nostrils just in case. A terrible few seconds passed until he could conclude that the flow had been stemmed, at which point he immediately slipped onto the floor next to Orlando. "What should I do, Mrs. T? Will he be all right?"

"Of course he will, love. Just give him a moment. It must have been the shock of seeing that blood everywhere made him pass out. Is he on the squeamish side?"

"Not that I'd ever realised. He gets a bit upset sometimes if he thinks I'm in distress." He remembered the temper tantrum thrown at a rugby game, where Orlando had been convinced that Jonty was going to be killed in every tackle. "Bit of a mother hen, I'm afraid."

A slight groaning noise indicated that mother chicken was coming round. Jonty encouraged him to sit up, while Mrs. T fetched a cup of water. "Here, ducks, have a little of this." She fussed over him as if he were her own son.

"What happened?"

"You fainted, old chap." Jonty placed his hand on Orlando's shoulder, as brave a gesture as he could manage, even though they had no real secrets from their guest.

"No, not that. I knew I fainted, it's happened before, after a rugby game. I mean your eyes."

"Oh, my nose is just a bit too small for efficient first aid, it sends the blood the wrong way sometimes. Mama fainted the first time she saw it, too. Sorry, I should have warned you."

Orlando produced a wan smile. "Bit of a shock to the system." He turned to Mrs. Tattersall. "I'm sorry if I caused you any trouble."

"Oh, don't fret about that. Dr. Stewart came to get me because he was so worried and needed a bit of reassurance. I was only too glad to help, I've seen many a nose that wouldn't stop bleeding, my father being a doctor." She smiled to see the discomfort of a robust young man for whom such spectacular bleeding was a distinct source of concern. "Now, I'm going to ask Mr. Greenwood to have your dinner sent up on a tray tonight, and I shall make sure it's got beef in it, with a nice bottle of red wine on the side. Need to build you both up." She reached out her wrinkled hand and pinched first one man's cheek, then the other's. "Daft pair, you are."

Once she had departed, full of *things to be doing* which was obviously her delight, Orlando grabbed Jonty's hand. "Thought you were dying. Never seen anything like it. Made a bit of a fool of myself."

"Nonsense, Orlando. I'm just concerned that you're well—shock can be a terrible thing, Father says people can die of it. Oh, I say, perhaps mentioning that wasn't very sensible, you look all pale again." He squeezed his lover's distinctly clammy mitts. "Think we could do with a nice cup of tea before dinner, not a stiff drink—I think that would do you more harm than good. I'll ring for the maid." He rose, but Orlando pulled him back.

"No, don't go..."

"It's only as far as the bell pull."

"No, not yet. Can't be without you at the moment." His eyes began to well—the flow of tears, once started, couldn't be stemmed as easily as Jonty's nose had been. "Really did think you were expiring, and it would have been all my fault. I've been such an idiot this holiday. Such an idiot all my life."

"Now, now. Less of that." Jonty produced the only hanky he had to hand, a rather sanguine one, to attempt to wipe his lover's face. "Sorry about this, but it's the only cloth I can get hold of until you let go of my paw. Hope the laundry returns some of these soon or we'll be in terrible trouble. Gone through a few today."

Orlando produced a rather wan smile at Jonty's indomitable spirit. "Thank you. Perhaps I could let you go as far as my drawer to get another one or else my face will end up as smeared as yours. We must look like Roman gladiators or something equally bloodthirsty."

"Dare say we do." Jonty's voice reached through from the other room. "But I don't care at this particular moment. Here you are." He proffered a clean cloth. "Can I go and sort this out?" He indicated the bloody flannel, waited for his friend's nod, went off to rinse it, then brought it back to use on his streaky face. "Just a bit of mess, eh?" Jonty looked down at the carpet, where little red drops, eluding his hand, had left a strange pattern. "Bit gory that. Looks like my room did after..." He stopped, not wishing to carry on with the inevitable next parts. Student. Throat. Razor.

"Not as bad as then. Even that wasn't as gruesome as our dining table when my father did the deed."

Jonty looked up in surprise. It had taken him months to winkle the true story of Coppersmith senior's death out of his son, at a great cost, and now Orlando was talking of the event very calmly. He smiled, putting his arm around his friend's shoulders. "All better now."

"No, it isn't. It'll never be better until..." Orlando tipped his head towards the bedroom. "And you can't sort that out as easily as pinching your nose."

"I can't, but you can. I've realised the solution lies in here." Jonty stroked his lover's head. "That's why I can't lay my hands on it. Lost among all your childhood memories. Sort it out—conquer it like you conquered your inability to tell me about your father."

"Easier said than done." Orlando blew his nose again.

"Of course, but that's what makes it worthwhile." Jonty couldn't help giggling. "I'm glad the dunderheads can't hear me—I sound less Hamlet than Sunday school teacher. We'll overcome this, calculus-britches, you'll just have to find the next logical step."

A kiss would have been the next logical step and certainly would have happened had Matthew Ainslie, with his immaculate timing, not come to knock on the door.

The men shared a look of mutual regret and then called for Matthew to enter. His handsome face came round the door, saw the scene of carnage then raised an eyebrow. "Have you two got fed up with each other and decided to fight it out over fifteen rounds? I'd offer my services in your corner, but I can't do the job for both."

"Suppose we do look a sight at the moment, Matthew. Orlando decided to play a schoolboy prank which ended up giving me the king of all nosebleeds. Then to add insult to injury, he fainted and left me to get help. Idiot." He gave his friend what he hoped looked like a glare, but Matthew must have seen the affection in it.

"I'll go, shall I?" Matthew looked unsettled, like someone who realises they're an uninvited guest upon hallowed ground.

"No, not at all. We have a while before dinner, which Mrs. Tattersall is at present insisting we have served in our rooms. If you can stand the sight of exsanguination—" he indicated the carpet, "—you're welcome to stay."

Matthew perched on the edge of a chair, still awkward. "I'd hoped to share a little bit of information with you, but if it's not convenient...?"

"Matthew, how many times do we have to tell you that it's perfectly fine. Isn't it, Orlando?"

Orlando had recovered some colour and nodded fairly positively. "Any time is convenient if it's news related to this ghastly business."

"I believe it is, as it concerns Alec, the barman. I understand he's denied everything to the authorities, who've been left to try to find a way to link him either to the letters or my father, if not to the murder." His eyes took on a steely glint. "I have a link."

"Tell us." Jonty's eyes matched his gleam, twinkling like the stars which would soon grace the summer's night.

"My little pal Alice. She's not daft—my questions, and le Tissier's, have given her pause for thought. Where do you think she saw Alec Banks on Monday morning?"

"Coming out of your father's room?"

"Absolutely, and she hasn't seen fit to share this with the authorities yet, only me. She thinks that because it doesn't accord with the time of the killing, she doesn't have to tell them, but I think it's an interesting little titbit."

"It is indeed," Orlando now had the scent of the quarry. "What time was this?"

"After breakfast, while we spoke on the terrace—my father had returned to his room to complete his ablutions. There would have been no legitimate reason for Alec to have been there, as far as I can recall."

Orlando beamed. "It's more than an interesting titbit, Matthew. It's downright fascinating."

"There's more." The brightness in Matthew's eyes faded. "She's got sharp ears, that girl. It seems she overheard your friend Inspector Wilson talking to his brother-in-law."

"And?"

"It appears they feel close to making an arrest."

Orlando felt thwarted. "Banks? Did they know where he was on Monday?"

"Not Banks. Me."

Chapter Twelve

"One of the last chances we'll have to do this for a while, Jonty."

It had been Orlando's turn to bring his early morning tea into the room where they'd spent the night—a late one, after they'd tried to convince Matthew Ainslie that even if he were arrested, they'd make sure he was cleared. Or at least Jonty had assured him; Orlando couldn't quite quell the thought that this man had been playing a nice little game of double bluff with them. He was an impassive player at the bridge table—perhaps he used those skills of dissemblance elsewhere.

It had proved a hot, humid night, with windows wide open and not a breath of air to be had. They'd abandoned all forms of nightwear in favour of what Jonty called his "birthday suit", a term which had never been employed in the Coppersmith household. His mother had tried to better herself, had sought to act and dress as the gentry did, but she would have been astonished at how the Stewarts led their lives. There was more light and life in that family, yet fewer airs and graces, than in a dozen others combined.

As for the Sunday school notions that Mrs. Coppersmith had tried to drill into her son's head, they'd seemed to entirely consist of great lists of things which were not to be done, implying that the only way to live as a true Christian gentlemen was to be miserable all the time and to regard anything in any way pleasurable as sin. Charity was only to be given to the deserving, those who conformed to your own narrow viewpoint. God was the one from the Old Testament, all vengeful judgment. It was no wonder that Orlando had lost any faith he'd ever possessed so early on in life.

Jonty had been, again, the source of revelation here. The Stewarts were a devout family, but "thou shalt not" was rarely heard, despite Mr. Stewart's assertion that the Ten Commandments were the basis for life. "Thou shalt" was used frequently. Mrs. Stewart had instilled into her brood that they should be civil to everyone, from the highest nobility to the beggar in the street. That there was no point in having wealth unless some of it was shared with people who were less well off and not just via the route of sending the Ascot bookies home happy. That there were plenty of things in life given to be enjoyed—if you didn't get stuck in and make the most of them, then you'd have a lot of explaining to do come the day of judgment.

Unusual, refreshing, controversial, yet all of it based on knowledge of scripture that astounded many people who should have known better. Mrs. Stewart seemed to have entire chunks of the New Testament off by heart and wasn't afraid to quote it mercilessly. Orlando had seen a Methodist minister, an ardent teetotaller, reduced to tears by the sermon he was given on how the Bible not only condoned drinking but on some occasions positively encouraged it. Mrs. Stewart had cited chapter and verse until the man had bleated his surrender.

Not for the first time Orlando indulged in his private fantasy that he'd been adopted into the Stewart household as a baby. He pictured himself as a waif left on the doorstep, Mrs. Stewart being totally enamoured of foundlings, orphans and unfortunate girls who'd been led up the garden path then left in the family way. He would have been taken in, raised as one of the brood, given a childhood happy beyond all measure. He

185

could have been at school with Jonty so could have protected him—Orlando was convinced that between them they would have seen off the predators, no matter how unrealistic that conviction was. Maybe they'd have been at university together, perhaps the same college, perhaps sharing rooms. It was a fantasy beyond all compare, especially with the holidays, excursion after excursion, days without number of beaches and fields and getting into trouble.

There was only one problem with this dream world, apart from the fact that it had never, nor would ever exist. Jonty would have been his brother and while there would have been no biological link, the likelihood of their indulging in a romantic liaison became much reduced, all sorts of taboos being invoked, despite the lack of common parents. But the fantasy remained, being taken out for an airing on occasions he needed a bit of comfort, such as now.

"Lost in thought are we, Orlando? Formulating some wonderful new theorem about the square roots of negative numbers?"

"I was actually thinking about the lady I love." It was a deliberately provocative remark, one which produced the desired effect of Jonty spilling his tea down himself. "I mean your mother of course," Orlando continued, with an insouciant air.

"Miserable bugger, you did shock me there. Thought you were going to produce some ghastly revelation about a college servant with whom you'd produced a child on the wrong side of the blanket."

Orlando answered with a contemptuous snort. "Look at the state of your face." Jonty's nose had bled again in the night and his face still bore streaks of dried blood. Orlando gently wet his hankie with a bit of saliva, tenderly wiping it away.

"Well, that's a trick you've learned off your fancy piece, if I can take the liberty of referring to Mama as such, as she's a

great one for the spit wash. Still does it now if she catches me."
Jonty flinched as a particularly wet piece of cloth dabbed at
him. "Would you leave off, please? I am not a kitten to be licked
by its mother."

Orlando smirked. It was a look full of naughtiness and
what might just have been lust. Whatever it meant, the gaze
was more lascivious than normal.

"Now that's an exceptionally good idea, Jonty." He leaned
over, applying his tongue to his lover's cheek. "A bit like licking
sandpaper at this time of the day but not unpleasant." He
began working his way down to the neck. "I think this bit is
ridiculously dirty."

Jonty squirmed and giggled, excited out of all measure by
this display of stupidity. "Orlando, if this continues, it might
have the most untoward consequences. What if the maid then
comes in to get the cups, thinking we've gone to breakfast?"

"Don't care. Let her." Orlando had found the piece of flesh
above the collarbone which drove Jonty wild when it was
kissed. But it did him no good; his advances were still being
rejected.

With a laugh, Jonty threw him off, whacked him with a
convenient pillow then took himself off for a wash with a flannel
rather than a tongue. Not, it has to be said, without a secret
touch of regret.

The day promised to be fair again—they couldn't believe
their luck with the weather this holiday—so they plumped for a
leisurely walk into St. Aubin to view the fishermen, followed by
an equally leisurely stroll back to the hotel for a spot of lunch
before taking a cab across the island.

The cab ride never happened, as lunch was followed by the
arrival of Wilson and le Tissier. They conferred with a worried-
looking Greenwood, then came over to the young men, confiding
that both Mr. Ainslie and Alec, the barman, had gone missing.

187

This pair had been spotted conversing in a heated manner after breakfast, but at lunch the barman had failed to report for his shift and was nowhere to be found in the hotel or grounds. Matthew, too, was in none of his usual haunts.

Wilson was fairly certain that his old friends might have light to shed on the matter. "Gentlemen, if you have any ideas about these mysterious disappearances, I beg you to share them with us. You don't want to be accused of hampering police enquiries." The inspector smiled, but there was no warmth in it.

"Matthew—Mr. Ainslie—told us last night that he had been talking to Alice. She told him that she'd seen Alec coming out of Ainslie senior's room on the morning of the murder. We assumed he might have gone off to tell you all about it, but I suppose..." Jonty tailed off. It was a pretty weak assumption.

"He has quite a habit of taking things into his own hands, doesn't he, our Mr. Ainslie? Rather like you two." Wilson's voice had a cutting edge. "Had you worked out that we were about to arrest him?"

Orlando answered, "No," just as his lover said, "Yes".

Le Tissier let them stew a moment before he spoke. "Which is it, then? Yes or no?"

"Both." Jonty took charge. "We hadn't worked it out, but we did know. Matthew told us last night and he was pretty cut up about it."

"You seem to have a habit of getting yourselves incarcerated with killers, proven or suspected."

Orlando bridled "That's unfair, Mr. Wilson. We could no more have shut ourselves off from the students at St Bride's as we could have evaded Matthew here. Not if we wanted to still prove useful to you, as requested. We never deliberately set out to put ourselves in danger."

"Not even when you went straight to Dr. Stewart's room to intervene when you realised his life might be threatened? Don't you describe that as putting yourselves at risk?"

Orlando had turned very cold, detached. "No. I call that trying to protect a very dear friend and colleague, as you might have done for the inimitable Mr. Cohen."

A standoff having been reached between the two men, open hostility wasn't far away. Le Tissier intervened. "Gentlemen, it would do us no good at all to rehash all our old cases and whatever shortcomings were revealed in them, if we were then to commit the error of letting another killing occur." He turned to Jonty. "I only hope that you and your colleague don't end up being accused of aiding and abetting a murderer."

Wilson cut in before Jonty could reply with either word or fist. "We can surmise that Mr. Ainslie believes Alec knows something about his father's murder—it sounds as if they've already had words on the matter. Perhaps they've gone to talk this out somewhere they can't be overheard or overlooked. In which case they are both probably at risk—there will be no love lost and feelings running very high. I suggest that we confine our efforts to ascertaining where they might be. Can you enlighten us?" He turned to Jonty.

"I can't, I'm afraid. Don't know where Matthew's haunts are." Jonty smiled rather ruefully. "Why not ask Mrs. Tattersall? Matthew always says she knows everything."

They consulted the great oracle of the Beaulieu, who, after a moment's reflection, speculated that he might well have gone up along the path through the woods by the tennis courts. "I believe it brings you out on a rough piece of land which stretches away all along to St. Brelade's bay. Mr. Ainslie has often gone up there, since his father died—he told me it helped him to think."

"That would be right." Le Tissier nodded. "It's open heath to the north and the cliffs to the south. There are plenty of places where people can sit and think undisturbed. You'd be well warned of anyone who approaches."

Wilson looked rueful. "Sounds like the ideal place to talk without being overheard."

        📖

"You've money enough to spare, Mr. Ainslie, anyone can see that. Bit of cash coming my way wouldn't hurt you, would it? It'd mean the world to me, get me set up in my own place instead of having to bow and scrape every five minutes." Alec Banks had met his adversary—or was it victim—as agreed, up on the barren heathland where hare's-tails whipped at their legs.

Matthew felt particularly grim. "If you'd come to me with a business proposition, in search of a bit of capital to set up your own project, I'd have been more than willing to listen. I like a bit of enterprise, and I'm all for encouraging it. But demanding money with menaces is quite another matter. My answer on that front is no. Always would be."

"Shame that I'll have to go to the police about it, then. It'd be terrible to see you up in court for such a dirty little crime." Alec scowled. "Ought to be ashamed of yourself. People like you are the lowest of the low. Perverts, that's what I'd call you, and you'd get a lot more than two years' hard labour from me, if I was the judge." He spat on the ground, grimacing. "It's a disgrace. Nasty little buggers like you rolling in it while decent blokes like me have to scratch around to earn a living."

"I'd hardly call blackmail decent." Matthew was icily cold in his speech. "Nor snooping around among other people's property, reading their letters, or killing their fathers."

"Your father." With a snort of contempt, Alec was ignoring all accusations in favour of his own narrow line of thinking. "He was no better than you. You should have heard what Mr. Sheringham was telling everyone about him that Sunday night.

Hardly a good example."

Matthew coloured. Heaven knew he was aware his father was no saint, but he wouldn't hear him vilified so, not out of the mouth of the man who had probably killed him. "You'll take that back, or you'll get the taste of my fist. Then we can discuss why you were coming out of our room that Monday morning." He saw Alec blanch, knew that he was getting somewhere. "Were you fixing up a time to come back and confront him? Giving yourself time to go fetch a blade?"

The other man still didn't deny the accusations about the murder. He was either so fixed on his own notions of inequality and unfairness that he was oblivious to all else—or he was guilty as sin. "Who said I'd been to see him?"

"Your friend Alice. She saw you, but she's been misguided enough in her loyalty not to share the fact with the police. But she did tell me and I'd like to know exactly what you were up to."

Alec smirked. "I was just having a little word in your old man's ear. I thought he might be prepared to cough up a little contribution to my funds, but he was as hard-nosed as you are. Tight-fisted, the lot of you, and us poor workers left to put up with the scraps."

Matthew exhaled loudly. Banks's constant theme of unfairness, injustice and his own self-righteousness was beginning to really madden him. "So you decided to come back later to apply a bit more pressure?"

"Should have done. Should have squeezed the pair of you till the pips squeaked."

Matthew advanced on him, fury mingling with the desire to avenge his own. "You'll tell me here and now whether you killed my father. Then we'll find Mr. le Tissier and you can tell the same to him."

Alec laughed. "Want to fit me up for what you did yourself,

191

do you? You're not going to con me like that, Mr. Ainslie. Think I'm stupid or something?"

"On the contrary, I don't think you're stupid at all, I think you're very clever. You very nearly got away with murder, and that takes some doing."

"I dare say it does, but it takes one to know one, as they say. Same as whoever wrote those letters about you to Sheringham. I bet he was a man with a touch of the Sodom and Gomorrah, so he recognised another. Perhaps he was one of your friends, Mr. Ainslie, one of those you treated nicely, were free with your money around."

Matthew started, violently. All his life he felt he'd been holding part of himself in reserve, and very efficient he had been at it. Now that Alec had cut too near to the bone, got uncannily close to the reality of the letter writer's identity, he couldn't help but react. He grabbed the man's lapels, shaking him roughly. "You'll tell me right now why you killed my father. This charade has gone on for far too long."

Alec wasn't a weak man, but he couldn't match the formidable grip which Matthew possessed, struggle as he might. "I'm not telling you anything, not till you get your filthy bloody mitts off me. Dirty bugger, don't you touch me. I could catch all sorts of stuff from you."

Matthew tightened his grip, pulling Alec towards him. A sudden shout from behind—an instantly recognisable voice— caused him to jolt and the man pulled free. Matthew made a wild grab, too late to stop his adversary bolting up the slope towards the cliff path.

"Mr. Ainslie," Wilson called again, "that's quite enough. We have him in sight."

"He'll get away, man. Do you want to lose hold of a murderer?"

"I think that unlikely. Mr. le Tissier is coming along in the other direction with some of his local lads." The inspector approached, only slightly breathless from his rapid ascent. "I have my backup here." He grinned, pointing to Jonty and Orlando, whom he'd easily outstripped despite his greater age.

When those two eventually caught up, the pursuit picked up again, their quarry clearly visible against the skyline. Alec was effectively trapped in a pincer movement between the two parties, the other of which could be seen approaching from the northwest. There was no path down from the cliffs, just sheer rock faces with jagged outcrops at the bottom which could tear a man in half. He couldn't help but come back towards one group or another, unless he suddenly acquired the power of flight.

"What has he said to you?" Wilson's age had at last seemed to catch up with him, making him puff slightly as they neared the cliff path.

"He admitted both the blackmail and seeing my father on the morning of the day he died. He'd been trying a little extortion on *him* too."

"The murder—what about that?" Jonty caught up, red in the face from too much activity after a large lunch.

"He's not denied it, but he's not admitted it, either. I honestly am no closer to knowing, though not for want of trying." Matthew suddenly felt as if the whole exercise had been hopeless. "I'm sorry, Inspector, I should have left this to the experts. Got rather carried away by the exploits of our friends here."

"Well, they're no great models for anyone to base themselves on, Mr. Ainslie. They nearly got themselves killed last time around, getting too close to the murderer."

Jonty grimaced. "I suppose we're never going to be allowed to forget that fact."

"Not until you stop putting yourselves at risk of repeating

it." Wilson suddenly halted, holding out an arm to make the other men do the same. Their prey had stopped walking and was clutching his ribs as if suffering from a stitch. His head was turning from side to side, taking in the two approaching parties.

"Mr. Banks! We only wish to speak with you. I beg of you to come here so we can talk about this sensibly." Wilson spoke as calmly as he could.

Alec shook his head. "Nothing to talk about as far as I'm concerned. If you want someone to question, start with that bloke next to you. Threatened me, he did. Waved his pistol at me."

Matthew wondered how Alec could have known about the existence of the gun. Either the servant who had found him threatening suicide had blabbed or the barman had done even more poking about than they'd realised so far.

Wilson smiled, shaking his head. "You'd be surprised just how visible you are up here—there was no pistol being waved about. Anyway, I believe the weapon you're thinking of is firmly in my possession." He patted his pocket.

"But you must have seen him grab me. He made all sorts of threats and accusations. Lies, all of it. I never done a thing wrong."

Wilson edged gradually forward, motioning with his hand for the others to stay where they were. A precarious point had been reached, the cliff edge looming perilously close for all of them. He hoped that le Tissier's keen sight would take in the situation and he would hold his forces back. Their quarry was frightened; a nervous man was much more dangerous to approach than a calm one.

"I never said that you had, Mr. Banks. We just need to clarify one or two things. There's a good chap." The inspector edged closer again, provoking his prey to move back. Alec was now uncomfortably near to the edge so discretion called for

Wilson to retreat.

He sneered. "Afraid of heights are you? Shame. Perhaps if I could just keep walking along here, you'd be too scared to come and get me." He looked over the edge. "Long way down. It'd be such a pity for your wife to see you lying at the bottom. Don't think anyone would survive it." A strange recklessness had overcome the man, making him edge nearer to the rather unstable ground at the very boundary of the cliff.

"For pity's sake, you'll fall!" Matthew could restrain himself no longer. He didn't want their quarry dead—he wanted to see justice done, even if it meant his name being brought up in court then smeared over the newspapers. He owed that much, at least, to his father.

Alec laughed, hollowly. "Bet you wouldn't really care if I went—" then, as if he read the other man's mind, "—means that you'd not be dragged through the courts. Keep your revolting little secrets to yourself then." He stabbed his finger towards Matthew. "Oh, to hell with it. You both needed it, the pair of you bastards. Deserved all you got and all that's coming."

He flung his arm out in a dismissive gesture, losing his balance then stumbling backwards. Wilson reached for him, a reflex reaction, no doubt, to stop him tumbling over the edge. He should have known this very action might cause what it hoped to avoid.

Alec jerked away from the policeman, lost his footing entirely on a crumbling piece of earth, and fell backwards. He plummeted like a stone, his body bouncing off the cliff face and breaking on the rocks.

📖

The news was brought back to the hotel by a very sombre party. The local lads were offered a beer in gratitude for their help, but Matthew and Jonty called for stiff whiskies all round, then were left to reflect on the afternoon's events. The police had already searched the dead man's room the previous day, but Alec's presence then hadn't made the exploration very easy. Sadder circumstances might provide richer pickings.

"I wish I had Sergeant Cohen here," Wilson said ruefully. "That man has a habit of nosing out hidden items. You'd be amazed where he's produced vital evidence from. He likes secret drawers and patent hidden safes or loose floorboards with a cache beneath." He nodded to Orlando, "Perhaps you might like to come with us to play his part?"

"I'd be honoured." Orlando, chest swelling with pride, felt like a boy who'd been given his school prize. Their detective skills were being truly acknowledged at last. Better still, he'd been asked and not Jonty. He hid the smile that was threatening to crack his face then followed the policeman up to Alec's room, where they began by gingerly testing the floor. In one corner, beneath where the bed had been before they'd dragged it out, the board wasn't safely nailed in place and could be easily prised up. Wilson did so, whistling with delight at the treasure trove it revealed. Two little books.

They had no solid evidence against Alec so far, except for Matthew vowing that the man had admitted to writing the blackmailing letters, and Alice's testimony. The little black notebook that had been so carefully hidden away under the floorboards changed that, albeit circumstantially. It contained, among some fevered writings, the detailed financial plans for a business venture. The first few drafts were vague, with much scribbling about rates of saving, then there was a clear plan, based on the investment of an amount which exactly matched that asked for in the first blackmail letter. A revision of this plan dealt with an investment totalling the sum requested in the second letter. More chillingly, there was a subsequent revision that appeared to be based on similar regular payments being made over a period of time. Alec's intention had obviously been, like so many blackmailers, to keep coming back for more, like the proverbial Dane for the Danegeld.

The handwriting in the book gave few clues, even if it matched that in the threatening letters. Some unusual misspellings, like *disgrasefully* for *disgracefully*, found in both the letters and notebook suggested the case was sealed. If Alice verified this was her Alec's writing, then they'd probably solved the blackmail case.

Now, they only needed to find a link to the murder. The words which Banks had spoken out on the cliffs, both to Matthew and to Wilson, had been analysed repeatedly to see if the full tale could be established, but the police remained unconvinced.

Le Tissier had hold of the second book. It was what was known as a "shilling shocker", a cheap little volume which contained "true" stories of crimes and misdemeanours. There were similar books on the bookshelf, this one alone being secreted. A little passage was carefully marked up inside it, concerning a woman who had killed her husband's mistress using one of his tiepins by inserting it into a similar spot to the one which had caused Ainslie senior's demise.

Le Tissier showed the book to the other men.

"Close, my friend, but not enough, is it?" Wilson shook his head in frustration.

"No, not for me, anyway. Perhaps for some of the more leaden-footed of your colleagues who feature in these." Le Tissier waved the sensational little book. "I want something much more tangible."

Orlando knelt down by the bed. "We could just see if the angels are smiling down on us today. I've a longer arm than you—I could have one more poke around in here." He produced several grimaces as he fished around for anything which was more than simply dust or a mouse dropping. His face suddenly registered success, as he pulled something white with rusty coloured streaks from the hole. "I think you might have just got your evidence, Mr. le Tissier."

In his hand Orlando bore a man's handkerchief which looked like it had been used to wipe a bloody stiletto at some point in the not-too-distant past. Embroidered in the corner was the initial *A*. For Alec.

📖

"I was right, wasn't I?" Jonty slipped off his dinner jacket and laid it carefully over the back of a chair.

"You were. Not Matthew at all." Orlando loosened his tie. "This time I'll have to let you win."

"Now that's exactly the spirit. Could use that sort of noblesse oblige on the croquet green, although I suspect that would be asking for too much." Jonty's own tie was soon flung over his jacket. "Hot again tonight."

"Sweltering." Orlando slipped his arm around his lover's waist. "Seems ages since we kissed."

"It is ages. Come here." Jonty smiled then leaned towards Orlando for a kiss, one which was given and received with much delight as they lingered in the embrace. "I've missed this."

"So have I." Slowly, in case of another rebuff, Orlando's fingers crept around to the small of his lover's back, tugging at the shirttail until it came free.

"So that's the way of things tonight, is it?" Jonty returned the favour; he was particularly fond of the skin at the base of Orlando's spine and liked to caress it at every opportunity, even if he didn't always compare it to an extinct giant armadillo's. These slow touches always seemed to be a prelude to more audacious things.

"It could well be, should we desire it enough. Unless Greenwood comes to the door to say that someone else is trying to kill themselves with a gun carrying no bullets or a knife with a blunted blade."

"If they do, I'll insist that we pretend we're not here. Let's put out the light just in case." They stood in the dark, close and warm, listening to each other's breath. "You do know there'll never be anyone else, don't you, Orlando?"

"Yes." He gave a huge, deep sigh. "We're one flesh, Jonty. We can't be put asunder by anyone, not Matthew Ainslie or Inspector Wilson or King Edward himself."

"Ah, there's the rub. Technically we're not one flesh yet, are we?" Jonty drew his hands up to the back of Orlando's neck, fiddled with the hairs there. "We could be, though, if you really did want it. If you were ready."

Orlando shivered. "I'll never be entirely ready. But tonight, I'm willing."

The sigh which went through Jonty's body would have made any reply unnecessary. "I've waited so long to hear that. What's changed?"

"I have no idea. I could logic it away and say it was the thought of the constraints put on Matthew by his father and how I was determined not to be under a burden from my parents, but that's a bit glib. I guess it's not wanting to disappoint you. No, ssh." Orlando's fingers stifled any argument. "I want this. Honestly."

Jonty kissed the fingers laid against his lips. "At least it won't be like it was for me—we'd only do it the moment you want to. Of course, it would be you doing the, you know..." He went bright red, and made a little gesture with his hands.

"Oh!" That made things less alarming. "I'd rather assumed it would be you..." Orlando made the same little thrusting gesture with his forefinger.

"Well, I hope it will be at some point, though I think perhaps we'd better start the other way round."

"Yes, I think I'd be happier with that, except I'd be worried about hurting you. During..." Orlando made the same little gesticulation. Now he was frightened again about his being inexperienced, the risk of being too rough or bringing back painful memories for his lover.

"Well, there are things one can do to make the process easier, comfier..." Jonty waggled his own forefinger again and the fit of giggles he'd been trying so hard to keep in check could be contained no longer.

Orlando laughed, too. *What a pair we must look. Grown men, unable to discuss such intimate matters without ending up like a pair of schoolboys.*

Jonty continued to waggle his finger, poking it into his friend's ribs, then into the waistband of his trousers. "I'm game, if you are."

Orlando put his arms around his lover, drew him in close. "Seems appropriate, doesn't it? I've tried all sorts of new things this last week or so." It sounded brave, or he hoped it did. He was still terribly unsure, but his lover wanted it and what Jonty wanted, *he* wanted Jonty to have.

They kissed, Orlando aware of his friend's probing little fingers starting to undo his shirt buttons. That was reassuring, this was how things usually started. Kisses, buttons; maybe the rest wouldn't be that different.

"There's an awful noise in here, Orlando." Jonty held his fingers to his lover's lips. "Oh. It's just your brain whirring again. Whatever you're mulling over, stop it." He kissed his lover heartily, passion growing with every movement of his tongue.

It felt as exciting as their very first kisses had, months ago, as if the fact that tonight would have a different ending made it a new beginning. Orlando started, between kisses, to strip off Jonty's clothes, each little layer of boiled shirt, socks, representing another step into the familiar and the unknown. He quivered with anticipation, steadying his trembling by holding his lover tightly against him once he was bare-chested. The well-known combination of muscle and flesh both comforted and excited him. "Come on, you take off the rest. I'm not sure I can manage trouser buttons."

"You are shaking a bit, aren't you?" Jonty caught hold of his lover's hands. "Look, it'll all be like it normally is, well most of it anyway. Just...just the conclusion will be different. It'll be lovely, I promise, just as lovely as you could imagine. Better than anything we've done." He drew his hand down Orlando's chest.

The thrill that shot along Orlando's spine promised more than even his lover's words had done. He couldn't trust himself to speak, so gave his assent with a kiss then began to tackle his own clothes, concentrating fiercely on shoelaces and socks, anything that would help him regain composure. There was a bubbling up of excitement which was progressing at such a rate that, if he wasn't careful, they wouldn't even get as far as the normal conclusion of things, let alone anything different. He breathed deeply, trying to relax, which was hard when he kept catching the sight of Jonty undressing.

They'd decided that Jonty's bed was perhaps the more discreet, his room being right on the corner of the hotel, so they drew each other there, small steps and little nudges alternating with kisses, caresses, sighs.

When they reached the bed, they found the sheets were newly changed. The linen felt cool and stiff; it smelled subtly of the washing line. Orlando found the feel of freshly laundered sheets incredibly sensual, his skin delighted by their cool textures, the virgin state of the bed. If anything could add to the perfection of the night, this was it.

It began as it always began. Kisses, caresses, tender murmurings and whispered jokes, Jonty on the verge of giggles as he often was when they made love. Orlando felt the need to swat him at one point, insisting that his friend could do with having some sense slapped into him. He made sure it was the gentlest cuff possible. Excitement mounted, bodies tingling and readying themselves, so familiar each with the other, yet always finding new things to amuse or amaze.

Orlando was continually surprised at the novel delights he found in Jonty's bed, how the man could devise so many ways to make him writhe with joy, laugh in ecstasy. As they moved together now, flesh on flesh, mouth on mouth, a small sliver of fear crept up his back again at the thought of the unknown into which he would soon be plunged.

"Say no now." Jonty's voice was unnaturally hoarse. "If you've any second thoughts, it would be best if we just carried on as we normally do."

"No. I mean yes." Orlando nuzzled against his lover's ear, suddenly emboldened, in spite of his fear. It was now or never; if he balked at this fence, he'd never have the courage to attempt it again. "I mean we should."

When he felt Jonty's blissful sigh, he knew he'd made the correct decision. That opinion didn't change, even when Jonty proceeded with a string of tasks, finding a towel, scrabbling about in a drawer for something, tasks which weren't usual when they made love. Orlando wasn't so naïve that he couldn't guess why Jonty produced a jar of petroleum jelly—it was quite logical.

"It'll be more dignified if we arrange to face each other." Jonty spoke as tenderly as if he were whispering the sonnets. Then all was left to gestures or movements, two bodies finding each other anew, delighting and surprising one another until they became one.

Orlando couldn't believe how wonderful it felt, how it

exceeded anything he'd ever known, any pleasure he'd ever experienced. All his fears were proved to be unfounded—they seemed so stupid now, he really should have known better. If Jonty said that something would be lovely, then of course it would be. And this was far beyond lovely. The burst of unbearable ecstasy shattered him, made his body feel like it was being torn apart, then he felt simply wrapped in warmth and joy, a tender glow replacing the fires which had burned only the moment before.

"Thank you," Orlando whispered against his lover's neck, when he'd regained the ability to speak anything that resembled sense. "None of this would have happened without you. I'd never have even kissed anyone, all my life, if you hadn't come along. You've changed the whole world for me."

"You're a big soppy pudding, Orlando, and you're more precious to me than anything I've ever known. That includes Richard—I never loved him like I love you. Always thought of him as someone who looked after me. I prefer to be with my equal."

"There's something in the prayer book about becoming one flesh, isn't there? Then there's another line about 'with my body I thee worship'." Orlando laid his head on Jonty's chest, not wanting to be out of contact with him, even for a moment.

"Yes, Orlando." Jonty smoothed his lover's dark curls. "Why do you ask?"

"Because it feels like what we've just done has been about that. Can't explain very well, I'm not religious, you know that, but it's as if I've found something almost sacred. It's not dirty or nasty, like my mother said, or evil like some of the preachers make out, the 'sins of the flesh' and so on. Well, I could imagine it might be evil, if one of the people didn't want it." He stopped, conscious that he'd touched on Jonty's past.

The man simply hugged him, saying, "It's all right, carry on."

"I don't think it would mean a lot if we didn't love each other, like people who just do it for money. It can't be the same, can it?" He looked anxiously at Jonty, who this time shook his head.

"Not the same at all, Orlando. This is very special, the joining of souls, not just bodies." He sighed and held his lover closer. "We can't be put asunder now."

Chapter Thirteen

On Friday the two fellows of St. Bride's—who had arrived on Jersey pale and wan, it having been a disappointing summer in East Anglia—came down to breakfast looking brown and healthy, wearing huge smiles. They exuded goodwill to all men, even managing a bit for the "Misses". The day having dawned without a cloud in the sky and just the faintest of sea breezes coming in across the little harbour, Orlando was determined their last day should be spent in *their* little cove along the cliffs. There was no more investigating to be done, something he actually felt a tinge of regret for, especially as it didn't seem to be Mr. Honey Buzzards who'd been responsible. This only slightly dampened his enthusiasm. If he could have persuaded Jonty to miss breakfast—a crime of the first order in his friend's book—then they would have been in their bathers, in the sea, by eight thirty. As it was they bolted down their sausages, hitting the waves by half past nine. They swam, basked, lay on the rocks, and chatted contentedly.

"Let me get this absolutely plain. A lifeboat, a pumpkin and the giant rat of Sumatra?" When Jonty had begun to relate some strange tale of his childhood, Orlando had only been half listening so had only just picked up this strange combination of elements which had entered the story.

"I have to admit that, technically, it wasn't a giant rat nor was it from Sumatra, that was just a little fancy of mine based on Sherlock Holmes. It was a coypu belonging to one of our neighbours who was contemplating going into the fur trade and needed to see what the raw material was like." Jonty carried on without batting an eyelid as if these three things went together every day.

"Presumably you stole it?" Orlando decided he must just go along with the strange logic of the tale.

"No. To be precise, we just borrowed it for the day, as he was away in London and wouldn't have missed it for a week."

"You went to the coast?"

"Absolutely. Selsey Bill, to be correct, which isn't far from our country place, the refurbishment of which will be finished now, just in time for you to see it. Taken their time, but Papa says it was worth it. It's a glorious place, Orlando, in the middle of the rolling Sussex downs, not far at all from Chichester should you get the urge to visit the cathedral." Jonty grinned at the thought of his friend willingly expressing the desire to visit any such place.

Orlando snorted. "Don't change the subject. You and your brothers took this coypu thing down to the sea then put it in a lifeboat. Why?"

"Because it was *there*, right on the beach. We'd intended just to run the creature around a bit on a lead scaring the locals, as it was quite tame, if a bit fierce-looking. However, Sheridan saw this boat and thought it might like a journey out to sea. So off we went."

"Did it enjoy its little outing?"

"Sick as a dog. Worse than you coming here. And the mess stank to high heaven. We had to row back to shore against the tide—luckily we're all built like navvies—then try to clean the boat up. Cost us a pretty penny when the lifeboat man saw us. Well, it cost Papa a pretty penny in mollifying money, and we all had our backsides leathered. But it was worth every sixpence, every stripe." Jonty grinned.

"I still don't understand where the pumpkin came into it."

"Ah, that was 'acquired' en route for a threepenny piece. It was for the coypu's dinner and that's what we ended up scraping off the bottom of the boat. It wasn't pleasant."

"You still say it was worth it?"

"Oh yes, Orlando. Such a lark. If only you'd been there." He smiled wistfully. "If only you'd been born in Sussex in the little village near us. I'm sure your parents couldn't have disapproved of you wanting to be friends with the squire's sons. Then we could have had such wonderful times in the summer holidays— you would have ended up twice the size because Mama would have been continually feeding you up. My brothers would have bruised you black and blue like they did me." He suddenly stopped. "Oh, please don't cry. Please."

"Can't help it, Jonty, it's just what I would have wanted for myself could I have chosen."

Jonty put his arm round his friend, settling them back against the rocks, out of the stiffening breeze and out of sight of the rest of the world. "I'm sorry, my big mouth gets me into such trouble at times."

"No, it's fine, I shouldn't be so sensitive. It's just the end of our holiday is rearing its ugly head and I can't bear to think of us leaving here. Funny when you think of how reluctant I was to leave St. Bride's. Now I don't want to return there."

Jonty didn't speak, just tightened his grip round Orlando's shoulders.

"Truth to tell, I've felt like a child again here, only this time it's been happy. All the daft things we'll have to remember like catching prawns and rolling down hills. I really don't want them to end."

"Ah, there's always next year. Christmas and Easter holidays in between, as well. We can do whatever we like, go

207

wherever the whim takes us. Just imagine."

"I'll try to, but I just can't see how it will compare to this."

"Better than Margate or Ramsgate, eh?"

"Oh, there's no comparison. The company here is far better than my grandmother and her maids."

"Not a patch on Mrs. Tattersall, I bet. Your granny, I mean?"

"Indeed not, apart from the knitting. Grandmother Coppersmith is all black bombazine and starch. I can see her so clearly now, with her big bag of knitting, needles sticking out like Boadicea's knives. She always has letters everywhere, too—being written, being read, being opened by her great, ugly letter opener." He stopped abruptly, turning white.

"Whatever is the matter, Orlando?" Jonty dreaded another revelation about his lover's family.

"I've just had the most awful thought. I need a moment to follow it through." He sat contemplating, his face setting harder by the minute.

"It must be appalling to turn you that colour. Would you like to share it?"

He did, which made Jonty turn even paler than his friend. "You realise what this might mean?"

"I'm very much afraid that I do."

"Dear God, we need to talk to Matthew straightaway."

"I hope beyond all hope that I'm wrong."

"Oh, so do I."

The journey back to the Beaulieu was agonising, the walk along the cliff path seeming to take longer than it ever had before, all the time their minds racing. They'd assumed the murder had been solved, Alec Banks lying dead at the bottom of the rocks, waiting for the tide to be favourable to recover his body. He had surely taken his guilt with him, not just for writing the letters but for killing the man whose son had received them. They'd all accepted that Ainslie senior had decided to confront the blackmailer, with disastrous consequences. The stained handkerchief had been witness to it.

Perhaps they had got it totally wrong.

Orlando rushed into the hotel, enquired for Matthew, found him in his room packing some of his father's things, then dragged him bodily downstairs to the garden, where Jonty had located Mrs. Tattersall. They told him just to listen and be sensible, as they weren't sure but they had an inkling which, if it were true, meant the fat was in the fire.

"Hello, you young scamps. Now, why aren't you out making the most of your last afternoon here? You should be swimming or frolicking, not talking to an old woman."

"Mrs. Tattersall." Orlando assumed his most solemn and dignified face, reminding Jonty of how he'd appeared the first time they met. "Please would you tell us about your brother? How he died."

A wistful smile came over the lady's face. "Ah, I did wonder. My brother? He took his own life. The official report said it was a terrible accident with a gun, that he'd been cleaning it out and it had gone off accidentally, but that was all down to the friends he had—we had—in authority. It was suicide."

"Did he say why he had done it?" Jonty's voice was as soft as a cooing dove, coaxing Mrs. Tattersall through the difficult conversation, not that she seemed to need much coaxing. She appeared the least perturbed of all those present.

"He left me a note. Our friends kept quiet about that too, slipping it to me after the funeral. He said he'd been accused of cheating at cards, my Arthur, who never cheated at anything in his life, even when we were little children. It broke his heart. While he could have stood up to fight any accusations, he lacked proof of his innocence and couldn't see how to get any.

He couldn't face going through life with the shame hanging over him. Even if he'd been found not guilty, people do tend to say that there's no smoke without fire, which is such a very wicked saying. No smoke without the fire of people's jealousy and hatred, in my experience." She sighed heavily, put aside her knitting, rubbed her hands. "So he decided to end it all."

Jonty looked at Matthew, saw him shudder. Was he thinking of how close he had come to taking the same option?

"Mrs. Tattersall," Orlando broke the silence, a quietness heavy with deep thoughts, painful memories. "What was his name?"

"Arthur Featherstone."

"But that's..." Matthew suddenly sprang out of his thoughts and into the conversation.

"Yes, dear. That's the man your father accused of cheating. It was his charge which led Arthur to kill himself." The lady quite unexpectedly reached out to pat Matthew's hand, as if he were the one in need of comfort.

"Is that why you killed him?" Orlando spoke with no trace of coldness or malice in his voice, just calmly stating a fact as if he were discussing something with his students.

"I suppose it was, in the end. I hadn't intended to. Let me explain." The three men turned attentively to her, like little boys awaiting a story from their grandmother. She smiled at Orlando. "On that Sunday night when you were so very talented at bridge, Sheringham had been talking to my Aloysius over at the bar." She nodded to Matthew. "I think your father must have become aware of it, because he got very agitated all of a sudden. I think he might have heard the name Featherstone mentioned—Mr. Sheringham does have such a loud voice. Anyway, Mr. T told me all about it afterwards. I had only ever known the surname of the man who made the accusations against Arthur, nothing else about him, and Ainslie isn't uncommon, is it? I did so want to just speak to your father to see what it was all really about, set my mind at rest."

Mrs. Tattersall seemed suddenly very tired, not to mention breathless, so Jonty went off in search of a waiter and a pot of tea. She awaited his return before recommencing the story. "Sorry about that, my dears, I sometimes get a little drained. I suppose it's my age. I arranged to meet your father when you were playing tennis with Dr. Coppersmith. I'd heard you two out here making the arrangements, so it seemed like an ideal time. Well, I asked him straight out and he said that he had been the very man to catch my Arthur red-handed. Oh, it made my blood boil—as I've said before, my brother would never do such a thing."

The refreshments arrived, carried by a rather pale waiter, all the staff having received the most terrible shock when they heard of the barman's demise. Mrs. Tattersall was poured a cup of tea by the son of the man she had killed, something that could probably only have happened among an English gathering in an English hotel.

"I'm afraid your father wasn't very sympathetic, my dear. He didn't realise he was talking about my brother, I'd just said that Arthur was a young man I had known. He started to brag a bit, and while he didn't quite say as much, he implied it had been *he* who had been pulling a sharp trick or two at the tables, not Arthur. He seemed rather pleased with himself that he'd got away with it. He was sitting at the desk all the time. I had my knitting bag with me as usual and I suddenly remembered how sharp the thinnest needles are. I recalled my father telling me about the sort of places where it would be fatal to insert a thin, sharp blade. So I just did it. Straight into the back of the neck and up into..." She stopped, reached over as if to pat Matthew's hand again, then seemed to think better of it.

"I'm so very sorry, my dear." Mrs. Tattersall looked into his eyes with great pain. "I would have given anything not to hurt you, but I didn't consider anything else at the time. All I could think of was my brother and how much I loved him. And how unfair it had all been." As she started to cry, she was offered three differently monogrammed handkerchiefs simultaneously. The tears didn't last long, as Mrs. Tattersall was one of the old school, tutored not to show her feelings excessively. She dabbed her eyes then put on a brave face. "You're bright little buttons, aren't you? How did you guess?"

Orlando sighed. "It was today. I was thinking about my grandmother, who always carried her knitting bag around, as you usually do. I suddenly wondered why I hadn't thought of her when first we met, then I realised you hadn't got your knitting that first night. If you hadn't got your knitting, you couldn't have lost a needle then, could you?" Mrs. T shook her head while Orlando continued. "So if you hadn't lost the needle, why tell such a blatant lie? I don't think that your memory lapses, like other—" he searched for a polite term, "—more mature ladies. Then I remembered you saying how sharp your needles were. I wondered whether they were sharp enough to kill someone with, how easy it would be just to wipe them on a handkerchief and put them back into their bag. Mr. Tattersall is Aloysius, isn't he? So his hankies might well have an A on them."

Mrs. T nodded.

"It all fell into place then, such a simple theory to explain what had gone on, no need for 'multiplying entities' as Dr. Stewart calls it."

They all sat in silence, the solution of the day before thrown out and the world turned upside down once more.

Jonty looked from Orlando to Matthew then back again. "What now?"

Mrs. Tattersall blew her nose. "I'm afraid I'm not sure that I'll make it to trial, you know. Bit of a shame, really, as I'd like to stand up in court and tell the truth. Perhaps they wouldn't believe me, but at least I could try to clear Arthur's name. However, that's all a vain hope. The doctors say I'll just about live to see my great-grandchild and then that's it. Off to a better, fairer place, I hope. This was to be our last holiday—it's been a lovely one really, apart from..."

Orlando felt the time had come to break the gathering up. "Come on, Matthew, we need to find you a good stiff drink."

Jonty watched the two men walk over the lawn to the hotel, pleased to see his lover tentatively clap the other man on the shoulder and offer some words of comfort. He turned to Mrs. T and patted her hand. "I would never have believed you had the strength in these to do the deed."

"Well, it was odd. My old dad used to tell a tale or two about people who had almost superhuman force in a crisis. He'd known a frail little woman whose son got trapped under a huge cartwheel—she'd gone over and picked the thing off him as if it were a dandelion clock. Same thing happened to me, I could have taken on Samson at the time. But your friend got something wrong, you know. You can tell him later if you like, make him a bit less smug." There was no spite in the remark, it was as if they were two little children having a laugh on their pals. "It wasn't Aloysius's hankie, it was Arthur's. I've kept one freshly laundered in my knitting bag all these years. Never used it, which is ironic considering what happened to it in the end. I found that I'd lost it just this weekend. I'd had it in the garden in my knitting bag, blood and all, because it seemed wrong to wash it. That barman must have picked it up, kept it for some nasty little purpose of his own. Well it's all out in the open now. I'll have to find a vicar to confess it all, though I've made my peace with God about it."

They sat and watched the birds circling up over the woods. They were honey buzzards, Jonty suspected, which was beautifully poignant. It seemed only a few minutes before Inspector Wilson appeared by the hotel door then slowly crossed the lawn. Whether Orlando had summoned him, or he'd been in the offing anyway, or perhaps—as Jonty suspected—he had some sixth sense that alerted him to a confession, he was there at the appropriate time.

"Mrs. Tattersall, Dr. Stewart, I believe that you might want to talk to me."

They didn't, although they had to oblige. When the story was complete, a tale that they were allowed to tell with the minimum of intervention, Wilson nodded, not just to his companions, but seemingly to himself. "I was never happy that Banks had been responsible for everything. Neither was Mr. le Tissier. We've only been discussing today the preponderance of men with the initial *A* at the Beaulieu and how we'd perhaps have to look at them closely. It was going to prove a difficult exercise, what with people going home and the culprit apparently named." He considered. "Maybe it would be a lot easier if we just stuck to that. I can't see this coming to trial in the short term—surely it wouldn't serve any great purpose to open it all up again with no proper end in sight. As long as Mr. Ainslie would agree?"

Jonty rose. "I'll go and talk to him." He found Matthew with Orlando in the bar, with glasses empty and all conversation ceased. He plonked himself down at their side, explaining the rather unusual discussion he'd just had. "It's unorthodox, I know, yet it may be the best solution. Less chance of things coming to light in court, things which you'd rather not have known. Oh, I know the letters shouldn't be brought up at the trial, but you never know what people will turn up once they start prying into things."

"It doesn't seem right, Jonty," Orlando stared into his empty glass. "For all that the young man who's waiting to be picked off the rocks was a nasty piece of work, no one denies that, it would only be fair if he too received some sort of justice."

"Justice, Orlando? You want to talk about that? I can think

of two young men in particular who did a lot worse than Alec, and they're still walking around free. You know what I'm referring to, so I'll not bore Matthew with the details. Sometimes justice can't be served, she has to turn her blind eye and just let life go on. Would there be any use served in pursuing this? That only Matthew can decide. It's fair dealing for his father which counts, not for a blackmailer."

Matthew had been very still, contemplating his fingers as they lay motionless on the table next to his glass. "I would have justice for my father, but not at the expense of someone who has shown me more kindness than many of my so-called friends." He saw Orlando's frown then clarified himself. "I don't include you in this—you've both been more than sympathetic. Mrs. Tattersall has had to suffer injustice for one of her closest relatives, so perhaps there would be an ironic kind of morality if we were to leave the situation as it is. I can see no black-and-white case here. All solutions seem equally unsuitable."

"Then the murderer lies dead on the rocks." Jonty sighed, rising swiftly from his chair in his anxiety to deliver the verdict to Wilson. He stopped at the door then turned. "Will you join us for dinner tonight, Matthew? I understand the dance has been cancelled, so we'll be able to have an uninterrupted game of whist afterwards. Seems the proper way to end this holiday, being quiet and civilised."

📖

Ginger ale before the journey, that'll stop the sickness. It was the last thing Mrs. Tattersall had said to the young men before they set off for the boat. It was typical of all that they knew about her, concerned to the last with their welfare, just as she had cosseted and looked after Matthew Ainslie after killing his father in cold blood. But then she had felt no animosity towards the son—her concern for him had been entirely genuine. They felt a pang of regret in leaving her behind, to spend the last week of her last holiday in relative peace and with the prospect of new bridge partners arriving soon.

They left the Beaulieu with regret, too, having seen such happy times there. Now these were just memories to be taken out for airing when the days in Cambridge were long, cold and dark. The cove had been wished farewell the day before and Matthew had shaken their hands just before they boarded their cab.

"Keep in touch with us, old man. Addressing a letter to the college will get it there soon enough." Jonty beamed at their new ally.

"I'll do just that. I'll be following you home across the Channel once the business of an enquiry into Alec Banks's death is sorted. Le Tissier thinks it'll be straightforward, there having been plenty of witnesses to it. Perhaps we can meet again?"

"Of course." Orlando smiled then clapped him on the shoulder. "Just as long as there are no honey buzzards in the vicinity." It was a brave joke for him but they all saw the funny side.

📖

"Hit you hard this, hasn't it, Orlando?"

The voyage home was a quiet one, the Channel like a mill pond with hardly a ripple. The two fellows of St. Bride's stood all alone by the very rail where two weeks since Orlando had felt like the only welcome option was death. Now he seemed almost content with travelling and a wistful smile played on his lips as he looked back, straining to catch a glimpse of the islands.

"Aye, Jonty. I had such a fondness for Mrs. Tattersall, you know. A true lady, I thought her. Then to find out..."

"She was every part a lady. I saw so many qualities in her that my own mother has, like kindness, courage and an absolute need to stand up for those she loves. Put yourself in her shoes, my dear. Imagine it was someone that you held very precious who had suffered terribly at the hands of a third party, someone who was totally innocent."

"I wouldn't have killed over it."

"Wouldn't you? What if you met one of the men who hurt me at school? Could you really say that you wouldn't drive a spike into his neck?" Jonty looked at his lover closely, trying to penetrate through the veneer of reserve deep into the passionate heart and brain.

Orlando sighed. "You're right. I'd have done the same in the circumstances, perhaps much worse, especially if I felt he was gloating." He fingered his little onyx tiepin, staring down into the waves. "I keep having to learn again what it means to love someone beyond all reason. It makes you do irrational things, I suppose."

"Oh, I think Mrs. Tattersall was being totally rational. She would do it a thousand times over given the chance. Only human, like the rest of us."

They took a cab from the ferry terminal across to a little hotel in the middle of Southampton where they'd arranged to spend the night, before being picked up by the Stewart carriage. The contrast to the Beaulieu was amazing, harbouring a much more down-to-earth clientele, including one or two ladies who would have made the "Misses" blush. The smell of cigarettes and ale pervading the bars bothered the pair not a jot. They wanted only their beds, their own, single beds for once, being exhausted from the journey.

Southampton presented her most handsome face to them the next day as they took an early walk along the old walls, a blue mist over the water matching the colour of Jonty's eyes, the gulls mewing and swooping, the stones warm to the touch as they explored the fortifications. It was a perfect last adventure, rounding off a marvellous two weeks with a delightful morning.

They took a cab to the station and, when the train came, it was with a slight sense of regret that they embarked. They spotted the Stewart's footman long before they pulled into Chichester station and were escorted to a fine chaise, its pair of handsome chestnuts gleaming in the sunshine and straining at their reins.

They drove off northwards into the Sussex countryside, urban bustle giving way to little villages or farms. Parts of the area reminded Orlando of Kent, so he was lost in childhood memories until Jonty nudged him with a happy, "We're here."

The buildings were hidden by the impressive village church, meaning only a glimpse could be seen along the road that ran by the gatehouse, and that glimpse was of ruined walls. Orlando felt slightly disappointed, but as they came through the gate then drove along a bit, the road turned and the actual edifice came into view. He was stunned.

It was a castle, nothing less. For all that Jonty had waltzed around the subject, saying it was just a half-built property which his great-grandfather had acquired and done up a bit, a process which succeeding generations had continued, it could not be denied that it a was a castle. One probably dating back to Tudor times, if Orlando's slight knowledge of history was anything to go by.

They passed through the main portal into something that resembled one of the courts at St. Bride's, except for only having three sides, and no Cambridge college had ever had a chatelaine the equal of Mrs. Stewart, who came bouncing up wearing a floral patterned costume of dazzling hue.

"I thought you would never get here." She embraced Jonty with great force, smothering him in face powder which left patches on his bronzed cheeks, then turned her guns on Orlando. He was cuddled even before a word was said to him, leaving the man totally winded and incapable of reply. "Did they actually feed you at that hotel? Skinny as a rake as usual, but just in time for tea as is your wont. Apple cake—that's your favourite, I believe?"

Orlando managed a nod before they were led off to the library where Mr. Stewart beamed at them and immediately tried to whisk him off for a conversation on bridge, much to his wife's consternation.

"No, Richard, I won't have it. You can wait your turn. I've missed these boys enormously so I'm going to have my fill of them before I relinquish them to you. When they have told me about every moment of every day of their holiday—I got your postcard Jonathan, you really must improve your handwriting—then you can borrow Orlando." She beamed at her "boys" then began the inquisition, relishing every little detail, happily marvelling at their prowess both in the matter of swimming and in detection.

Eventually they were allowed time off for good behaviour and were taken to rest before changing for dinner, being led across the courtyard then up a little spiral stair. It was just like the ones in the turrets at Orlando's old Oxford college, making him feel exactly as if he were a nervous first year again. The butler opened the door of an imposing room, revealing a mass of ancient tapestries which had seen many a better day, original fireplaces, arrow slit windows facing out, newer leaded light windows facing in, and a huge four-poster bed against one wall.

"You are to stay here, Dr. Coppersmith. Your cases are already unpacked and the laundry in hand." The butler bowed slightly then smiled at Jonty, who almost counted as an old friend. "You, sir, are just next door." He led him across to a similar room that faced Orlando's across the narrow stone flagged corridor, leaving him to make himself once more at home

It wasn't long before a rapping came on the door, then Orlando's head appeared round it. He swiftly took in Jonty's apartment, grinned, took a run at the bed—another four-poster, this one with magnificent drapes—and leapt on it.

"It's been a wonderful holiday, but I'm glad we're home." He felt odd hearing the remark escape his lips, as he'd never been to the house before, could have no concept of the building as native soil. He'd previously invested all sense of belonging to a Cambridge college—now it seemed as if this loyalty had been transferred to a family. Orlando felt like a Stewart, a sort of fourth son, so where they were at home, so was he.

"Glad to be back too, it was a wonderful holiday, indeed. Now there's almost a whole year to plan the next one."

"Next one?" Orlando could feel an inane grin spreading over his face. "I keep forgetting there'll be more holidays, but of course there will." He lay back on the gloriously soft bedspread. "You plan them. I'm always safe in your hands."

"Of course you are." Jonty ranged himself alongside Orlando, placing his arm over his lover's chest in a gesture both protective and possessive. "Next year we'll go somewhere where there are no hussies to spy on us while we bathe." Jonty stretched, looking even more like a cat than usual. A great, golden cat, more lion than moggy, soft exterior hiding enormous strength and a massive heart.

Orlando found it impossible to believe he could ever love anything, or anyone, as much as he adored his friend. Not even differential calculus. "Jonty," he murmured, his thoughts turning in amorous directions until a sudden, chilling idea struck him. "Jonty..."

"Hm?"

"Next year, when we go to the place without hussies, can we go somewhere they don't have honey buzzards, either?"

About the Author

Charlie Cochrane's ideal day would be a morning walking along a beach, an afternoon spent watching rugby, and a church service in the evening, with her husband and daughters tagging along, naturally. She loves reading, theatre, good food and watching sport, especially rugby. She started writing relatively late in life but draws on all the experiences she's hoarded up to try to give a depth and richness to her stories.

To learn more about Charlie Cochrane, please visit her website www.charliecochrane.co.uk. You can send an email to Charlie at cochrane.charlie2@googlemail.com or join in the fun with other readers and writers of gay historical romance at http://groups.yahoo.com/group/SpeakItsName.

Orlando's broken memory may break his lover's heart.

Lessons in Discovery
© 2009 Charlie Cochrane
Cambridge Fellows Mysteries, Book Three

Cambridge, 1906

On the very day Jonty Stewart proposes that he and Orlando Coppersmith move in together, Fate trips them up. Rather, it trips Orlando, sending him down a flight of stairs and leaving him with an injury that erases his memory. Instead of taking the next step in their relationship, they're back to square one. It's bad enough that Orlando doesn't remember being intimate with Jonty—he doesn't remember Jonty at all.

Back inside the introverted, sexually innocent shell he inhabited before he met Jonty, Orlando is faced with two puzzles. Not only does he need to recover the lost pieces of his past, he's also been tasked by the Master to solve a four-hundred-year-old murder before the end of term. The college's reputation is riding on it.

Crushed that his lover doesn't remember him, Jonty puts aside his grief to help decode old documents for clues to the murder. But a greater mystery remains—one involving the human heart.

To solve it, Orlando must hear the truth about himself—even if it means he may not fall in love with Jonty the second time around...

Warning: carries a three handkerchief rating. Contains sensual m/m lovemaking and men in kilts.

Available now in ebook from Samhain Publishing.

GREAT cheap fun

Discover eBooks!

THE FASTEST WAY TO GET THE HOTTEST NAMES

Get your favorite authors on your favorite reader, long before they're out in print! Ebooks from Samhain go wherever you go, and work with whatever you carry—Palm, PDF, Mobi, and more.

LaVergne, TN USA
07 October 2010
199974LV00004B/18/P